*Tending to Grace*

ALSO AVAILABLE FROM LAUREL-LEAF BOOKS

KIMBERLY NEWTON FUSCO

# Tending to Grace

Published by
Laurel-Leaf
an imprint of
Random House Children's Books
a division of Random House, Inc.
New York

Laurel is a registered trademark of Random House, Inc.

Visit us on the Web! www.randomhouse.com/teens

Educators and librarians, for a variety of teaching tools, visit us
at www.randomhouse.com/teachers

ISBN: 978-0-553-49423-5

Reprinted by arrangement with Alfred A. Knopf Books for
Young Readers

Printed in the United States of America

First Laurel-Leaf Edition September 2005

10 9

For Steven

We drive out Route 6 on a silent day at the end of May, my mother, the boyfriend, and I. We pass villages with daisies at the doorsteps and laundry hung in soft rows of bleached white. I want to jump out of the car as it rushes along and wrap myself in a row of sheets hanging so low their feet tap the grass. I want to hide because my life, if it were a clothesline, would be the one with a sweater dangling by one sleeve, a blanket dragging in the mud, and a sock, unpaired and alone, tumbling to the road with the wind at its heel.

But I don't say anything as we head east.

My mother is a look-away.

# 2

My teacher is a look-away.

I am a bookworm, a bibliophile, a passionate lover of books. I know metaphor and active voice and poetic meter, and I understand that the difference between the right word and the almost right word, as Samuel Clemens said, is the difference between lightning and the lightning bug.

But I don't talk, so no one knows. All they see are the days I miss school, thirty-five one year, twenty-seven the next, forty-two the year after that. I am a silent red flag, waving to them, and they send me to their counselors and they ask me, "When are you going to talk about it, Cornelia?" I curl myself into a ball and squish the feelings down to my toes and they don't know what to make of me so they send me back to this class where we get the watered-down *Tom Sawyer* with pages stripped of soul and sentences as straight and flat as a train track.

We read that the new boy in *Tom Sawyer* ran like a deer, while the kids in the honors class read that he "turned tail and ran like an antelope."

I know because I read that book, too.

Sam finishes reading; Allison begins. Up one row and down another we go like a set of dominoes, each kid taking a turn at reading aloud and me waiting for my morning to collapse.

" 'It was Monday morning and Tom Sawyer was miserable,' " Allison reads. " 'He was always miserable on Monday mornings because it meant he had to go to school.' "

The copy of *Tom Sawyer* they use for this class sits open on my desk. The one Mark Twain wrote sits on my lap. I match paragraphs to keep my mind on something other than my approaching turn:

"Monday morning found Tom Sawyer miserable. Monday morning always found him so—because it began another week's slow suffering in school."

Allison finishes and Betsy begins. We read aloud in this class because the teacher doesn't believe we read at home. And so I wait, my stomach rolling, a lost ship at sea. We may be reading *Tom Sawyer* for babies, but Betsy's voice, as strong and supple as a dancer, hardly notices. She skips along the tops of passive verbs and flies over the adjectives and adverbs that stack and pile up like too many Playskool blocks. When Betsy finishes, the teacher looks over at me and her eyes widen just a bit.

"Cornelia, will you be reading today?" Her voice pitches too high, too singsong. Kids turn around. Everyone knows she gives no one else a choice.

I shake my head and look at my feet.

I am a shadow. I burrow deeper within myself and pray that if the other kids don't see me, they won't talk to me. I pretend I am the desk, the book, the floor, and we all expect less of me each day. I try not to lose myself, but the shame of always looking at my feet beats me deeper and deeper into the earth, planting me as surely as my mother planted tulip bulbs one summer, facedown.

# 5

No one likes the new girl. Her name is Ruth. She wears the goofiest glasses I've ever seen. But I like her. I like the way she looks me in the eye when I tell her something. She is kind underneath those glasses and she smiles when I joke around. I want to tell her my whole life story in ten minutes, quicklike so the words tumble down fast and furious, like my mother's promises. But I don't know how to begin, so we talk about books, which is another reason why I like her so much.

We have just read *Oliver Twist,* me for the second time, and we are trying to figure out how Oliver survived on the gruel they made him eat at the workhouse. We've made a pact to live on gruel for one day, cold and without sugar, but unlike Oliver's, our portions are unlimited. Ruth has brought Cream of Wheat. I've brought oatmeal, and it sits like cold clotted gravy on my tongue.

The girls in the lunch line point to us. The empty seats

beside us are magnets. I concentrate on my spoon. I wonder if they'll notice our lunch. *How disgusting. How odd. How much of a loser can you be, Cornelia Thornhill?*

I stuff my bowl into my bag and push it into my back-pack.

"Hey, we're not done," Ruth says. Her back is to the girls; she hasn't noticed. I nod toward them. She turns and hides her bowl in her notebook and stands up to leave. She is sturdier than I, more of an eggplant to my celery stick. I am so hungry.

"Oh, don't go on account of us," says Eleanor, the tallest of the three, breezing toward us. She has had a perfect mouth from the beginning of time, one that never has needed—and never will need—braces. I stare absently into the crowded lunchroom.

"How are you today, Cornelia?" Eleanor takes her napkin, puts it on her lap, and ignores Ruth. I take my napkin and wipe my mouth.

I smile quickly and sip my milk.

"Did you get the last answer on the test?" Eleanor asks.

I shake my head. The other girls are snickering behind their napkins.

She tries again. "You didn't read again today. How come?"

I take another sip and shrug. Eleanor is waiting for me to answer. I take another sip and wipe my mouth. I start wiping my lips with each sip now, afraid something else horrible will fall out of my mouth. Seven, eight, nine times, I mop my mouth.

Eleanor laughs and then her friends laugh and when I can't listen anymore, I stand up and run out the side door of the cafeteria. The lunch aide hollers and the force of it follows me all the way to the street, where my tears mix with rain.

# 6

The boyfriend is there when I get home. My mother flicks away the thin wisps of whatever it is they've been smoking.

"Hey, Corns," she says.

I walk past them to my room.

"Why don't she never talk?" the boyfriend asks, the man with the brain smaller than my little toe, the kind of guy just made for watered-down literature.

I slam my door.

They don't ask why I'm home two hours early. You got a kid, you notice things. Send her to school. Make her lunch. Ask about homework. Simple as that.

A teacher told me I should be an honor student. "Imagine, *Wuthering Heights*. Where do you get all those books, Cornelia?"

This is what I should have said: I walk right out the door, as soon as my mother falls asleep on the couch. I walk past the other apartments in the projects, past the health center and the day care center and the sign at the entrance that used to say WELCOME TO HARDINGTON STREET, but now because of all the graffiti it doesn't say anything at all.

I climb on a city bus and get off at the library. No one pays attention to you in a library as long as you're quiet. They think a kid with a book is a good thing. That's how I ran around New York City with *Harriet the Spy,* wandered the Ozarks with *Where the Red Fern Grows,* went to prep school with *The Chocolate War.* I learned about sex from Judy Blume and about God from the Bible. Honor your mother, it says. I have to laugh over that. I really do.

## 7

I hear them talking that night. "Come on, babe, let's me and you go to Vegas."

My mother laughs.

"I'm serious, babe."

My mother stops laughing.

"What about Corns?"

"We can't take no kid to Vegas."

# 8

The boyfriend reads the car ads at breakfast.

I want coffee. Thick and strong, the mug filled halfway with heavy cream, two teaspoons of sugar, the way I make it every day. Sometimes I eat one of the Little Debbie cakes my mother hides at the back of the refrigerator, but most days I just drink coffee.

Since the boyfriend moved in a few months ago, empty beer cans pile up in the kitchen sink. I have to clear them out to brush my teeth because he broke the faucet in the bathroom. He doesn't twist the bag of coffee closed and he forgets to put the bag in the freezer to keep it fresh; it's on the counter in a crumpled heap beside the coffeepot. Beans scatter all the way to the stove. He mixes up my spice bottles, which I've been keeping in alphabetical order since my mother gave up cooking. Milk dribbles across the floor.

"Your ma and me think we'll head out to Vegas."

I spoon coffee into the filter.

"What you think of that?"

I pour water into the top of the coffeepot and turn the power on.

"Why don't you never answer me, girl?"

I reach up and pull my Frosty the Snowman cup out of the cupboard.

"I'm talking to you. Don't you sass me."

*Sass,* I want to point out, means talking back. I'm not talking at all.

My mother drifts into the room, wearing the boyfriend's pajamas, and slumps at the table, resting her head in her hands. The pajama sleeves hide a mascara line that cuts into the thin skin below her eyes.

"Leave her be, Joe."

"I was just asking what she thought of our trip. She won't answer me."

"She don't talk to nobody, Joe."

"She damn well better talk." He stands, but I am already out the door.

# 9

My mother does not believe in complicated goodbyes.

We pack and load the car by ten. My favorite books are stacked to the brim of a plastic milk crate. My mother leaves no time to return the library's copy of *Oliver Twist,* so I lay it on top. She doesn't bother to call the high school.

"They'll figure it out soon enough, Corns."

She leaves the kitchen table, the vinyl chair in the living room that I like to read on, all the heavy stuff. She puts the electric bill and the telephone bill on the counter and leaves no forwarding address. She leaves the door open.

"There ain't no room for all those books," the boyfriend says when I carry them out.

I ignore him and put the crate under my feet and look out the window as we drive away.

# 10

"Agatha's a little peculiar, you know." My mother turns around in the front seat and tries to catch my eye. "But you'll get along just fine. Here, have one of these little cakes."

I don't look up from my book. I'm wearing my black dress from the Salvation Army just because my mother hates it. I like the way the lace skips along the top of my boots, softening the meanness of everything somehow.

"Corns?" My mother's voice catches somewhere between her throat and her teeth. I wonder if she is having second thoughts. She should be having second thoughts. When you have a daughter, you don't dump her off somewhere. Parenting 101.

# 11

Turning to stone is hard work. First you have to let the anger climb up from deep within you and as it turns over and over and rises up through your chest, you have to clamp your teeth over it and push it back down. Then you sort of imagine yourself getting real heavy, folding over onto yourself, getting thick so nothing can reach the spot far inside that hasn't turned hard yet. And you know that if you get it right, you're not so afraid.

A few hours later the boyfriend pulls up in front of a house with clapboards looser than old skin.

"This it?" he says, rolling down his window and whistling a bit through his teeth. "You got the wrong place, Lenore."

I'm surprised by his concern. I'm wondering about my mother's memory, too. From the back of the car, I look out at windows set with tiny panes that bubble in the afternoon sun and at ivy growing up past a cracked front door and onto the roof. A bird swoops into the gutter.

"Come on, Corns," my mother says, opening the car door for me. "Bring your stuff." The boyfriend shrugs and turns up the radio.

I wonder when a Girl Scout last sold cookies here. Not for a while, apparently, because the hem on my dress catches the grass as we trek to the front door.

"It's not going to be for that long, Corns. Just till Joe and me get settled." My mother pushes some of the ivy aside and taps at the door. The skin on her hand is thin, translucent, like china held up to the light. I can hardly hear her knocks.

I watch another bird fly across the yard and land on the roof and then an old woman walks around from the back of the house. She is tall and straight, pale as vanilla pudding, with gray hair twisted into a braid and roped around her head. Binoculars thump against her chest. My mother jumps a little when she sees her. "Agatha."

"Tell him to turn that noise off." The old woman nods to the car, but her eyes are on me.

My mother looks unsure about what she should do. She takes a few steps forward (is she thinking of hugging the old woman?), then changes her mind and turns toward the car, leaving me standing with my crate of books at my feet.

I hold my breath and hope the old woman doesn't talk. I watch another bird fly to the chimney. The boyfriend turns the radio down. "Your phone isn't working," my mother says as she walks back to us. Then she giggles in her nervous little way that's nails on a blackboard to me. "I need someone to take her for a while."

The old woman doesn't say anything, and my mother, who trembles like a skinny sapling against this tall oak, stumbles on. "It ain't easy for me. Her father's gone. Joe says we can make a better start in Vegas. But it ain't no place for a kid."

My mother has run out of things to say. No one says anything for a very long time. I am comfortable with long pauses because I have turned myself to stone. Otherwise my knees would be buckling. I count eleven birdhouses nailed to trees all around the yard.

The old woman stares at my mother. "Something the matter with your brain, Lenore?" she says finally.

My mother puts her hand on my arm. I can feel her shudder through the sleeve of my dress.

"Me and Joe, we'll come get her quick as we can."

The old woman looks out at the Buick. Thick smoke pours out the exhaust pipe. Joe drums his fingers against the edge of the steering wheel. "You ain't pickin' them no better, are you?"

My mother looks down. The old woman looks over at me. I turn and look out at the fields behind her house that rise to pine-covered hills and then to a mountain in the distance. A church bell rings.

When the old woman takes her eyes off me and looks at my mother, I feel the temperature drop. "Get the hell out of here, Lenore," she says.

I step toward my mother, reaching for her. But she pushes me away and hurries to the car.

The old woman looks down at me with eyes as hard and gray as nickels. I don't feel them, though, because I am a stone.

# 13

"What's your name?" The old woman waits for me to answer, but I turn away.

I watch a dragonfly on a daisy, a beetle on a cobblestone. I think about the Yodels we bought when we stopped at the gas station and how the cream leaked out of the plastic package and I threw mine away after the first bite. I think about how I wanted a coffee but my mother said no. Think about anything, *anything else,* I tell myself.

"Don't you talk?"

I look away. My stomach rises to my chest. I know what's coming and tears puddle in my eyes. I swat at them, pretending a gnat has flown too close.

The old woman pulls what looks like a sugar cube from deep within the pocket of her overalls. She doesn't bother to pull off the blue lint, just pops it in her mouth. "Want one?"

I shake my head. I want coffee. But I don't say anything.

"There are those who'd say a girl who don't talk is a dimwit. Are you a dimwit?"

I shake my head angrily and look at my crate of books and

think about heading for the road. Or straight up that mountain.

"You know what I say?" the old woman asks. "I say that when you got a voice, you damn well better tell the world who you are. Or somebody else will."

I take a deep breath and that's all it takes for my throat to lock and I'm caught in the lonely place between what I want to say and what I can't.

"C-c-c-c-c . . ."

I stop and turn away. My heart is a truck skidding crazily inside my chest. I gulp air, trying to loosen the silent knot that pulls tighter, tighter. The old woman does nothing but pull another sugar cube from her pocket and crunch noisily. "We'll be bored as two pigs in a pen if I do all the talkin' round here."

Let her see my voice, then. Let her see my colors. Let her see the awful wound in my throat. "C-c-c-c . . . C-c-cornelia."

My legs shake and I don't bother to check if the old woman is a look-away because tears fall in front of my eyes now and I'm looking at my feet.

# 14

"Only God's perfect," the old woman says after a bit. "And sometimes I'm not sure about even that." She chomps another sugar cube, then hoists my crate of books onto her hip, carries it up to her front step, and kicks the door open with a bang.

"Come on in. I'll get supper on."

The door latch swings dizzily on one nail as I walk into the house, first into a small hall and then into a kitchen, long and narrow, with beams on the ceiling and wide boards on the floor.

"Sit down and rest a bit." She points to a kitchen table in the middle of the room, hidden beneath an assortment of lunch dishes and breakfast dishes and probably the meal before that. I stack some of the dishes and push them to one side and wipe off a chair with the back of my hand and sit down and notice enough cobwebs on the ceiling to string a kite.

"Well, let's see now," she says, unwrapping the binoculars

from her neck and flopping them onto the table. "How 'bout some tea?"

I don't want tea, of course. I want coffee. But I don't say anything.

She fills a pot with water and sets it on an old white stove, twice the size of the one in our apartment. "You can call me Agatha." She pulls a root from a pot on the counter and begins shaving slices from it with a large knife.

"I'm the sister of your grandmother. I guess that's right. But I don't bother too much with relatives. Most of them bore me to death. My sister, she's dead now, but when she was livin', she couldn't tell the upside of a turnip. How 'bout you?"

I shrug, unsure if I've ever even seen a turnip.

"Later on, if you decide on stayin', I could use some gardenin' help." She puts the root slices into the pot on the stove.

I don't know what to say to that, not that I would say it anyway, so I watch her slice a round loaf of dark bread. She cuts three fat slices and puts them in front of me along with a jar of something brown and sticky. I wipe the dust off the edge of the plate with my thumb as she pulls a wheel of cheese from the refrigerator and cuts a pie-shaped slice and hands it to me. I slather the bread with a quarter inch of the sticky spread. I close my eyes and bite.

Yeast and whole wheat flour mingle in my mouth with something sweet, heavy, and slightly bitter—not honey, but pretty good. The old woman looks over at me.

"Molasses," she says. "Ever had it before?"

I shake my head.

"Only one way to eat homemade bread—smothered in molasses." She dips her finger in the jar and scoops out a lump of molasses and plunks it in her mouth.

I check the cheese for mold and place a sliver on my tongue. A sharp, dry taste fills my mouth, much better than Velveeta.

She pours two cups of tea and sits one down beside me. She slurps at hers like a child eating soup. I watch her and then, daring myself, take a slow sip. The tea tastes the way it smells, very close to root beer.

"That's sassafras," she says. "It's good for you."

It's not coffee, though, I think. Agatha stops talking and we eat in silence. As dusk comes and the temperature drops, she drags two rocking chairs over to the fireplace and lights a fire. She sits down and watches the flames. I think about my mother and try to rock my anger out.

She has no toilet.

*How can anyone have no toilet? Is it legal to have no toilet?*

"I turned the pipes off," Agatha says. "I can't afford no plumber."

In the backyard, behind a chicken coop with several clucking chickens, sits an outhouse surrounded by a thicket of weedy lilacs. It has a plank door and a window that faces east. It tips to the left.

"This is my old girl, Esther. She's near a hundred, you know. Imagine her tippin' over with me sittin' inside. Now that would be a sight, wouldn't it? So I treat her real nice, give her a name and everything, so she holds herself up proper."

She laughs at the way I'm looking at her. "Never used an outhouse before?"

I shake my head.

"The only problem is late at night when it's real cold and you want to get out there and back in bed real quick. Other than that, it's pretty good. Lots of fresh air, anyway."

I can't imagine why anyone would want a window in an

outhouse. Anyone could peek in. And worse, I see as soon as Agatha opens the door, are the two seats, side by side. Who would want company in there?

At least she has a roll of toilet paper on the wall. It sits under a narrow strip of golden flypaper, nearly covered with a pepper shaking of dead flies.

As night falls, something cries out from under the refrigerator.

"Don't be worryin' none," she says when I jump up from my rocking chair. "That be the cricket. Keep you up at night, I 'spect, if you're not used to hearin' critters."

She walks over to the refrigerator and kneels down. "I ain't figured how it knows when it's dark. Crickets chirp at night. It must be dark all the time under that icebox, but he knows just when night comes because that's when he starts singin' for me. Quite amazin', if you ask me."

She laughs and stands up and refills our tea.

"Any c-c-coffee?" I ask.

"Never drink the stuff," she says, sitting back in the rocker. I bring my tea back to my chair and listen to the cricket and the sounds of our rocking.

Mostly, I want my mother. I want to run after the boyfriend's car and tell her I'd be no trouble in Vegas, no trouble at all. The boyfriend wouldn't even know I was there.

I picture myself running after them. I'm so close, I'm reaching out to my mother. But she is looking away.

Agatha hoists the window open in the tiny room that is to be my bedroom. A hole stretches across a quarter of the screen.

A full moon rises and I can see a slight outline of the mountain in the distance. I wonder, how far away is it? How long will it take to climb? I've always wanted to climb something that high, but could I?

A bed covered with a faded quilt straddles three wide and uneven floorboards. It tips off one leg when I drop my milk crate near the pillow. Agatha looks at the books. "You read all those?"

When I nod, she snorts. "No time for much of that around here." She pulls an army blanket from under the bed and throws it on top, causing the bed to rock.

"Do you like mushrooms?"

I shake my head no, absolutely not.

"Too bad. I eat 'em for breakfast, more often than not. Right good on toast, they are."

We are quiet for a few minutes while she tries to get the

light switch to work. "Don't know why your mother brought you here," she says finally. "I don't know nothin' about livin' with a young girl." She looks at me for a minute, waiting for me to answer, but I don't, so she points to a dresser. "Put your stuff in there if you want," she says as she leaves the room.

I look past her to the window. My mother will be back for my birthday; she always remembers my birthday, even when I have to bake the cake myself and wake her up to celebrate. She'll be back for my birthday; my fifteenth birthday, I tell myself. "It's in October," I whisper to the mountain in the distance.

I pull the quilt back, sending dust flying about my head. I notice a cobweb fluttering at the top of the window like a curtain.

That's when the loneliness settles deep. I open *Oliver Twist* and lose myself in its pages. Oliver survived without his mother. I wonder how.

I fill an old metal pail with water and scrub my room, top to bottom. I wash the floor, paying particular attention to the space under the bed, and I wipe down the window frame, flinging the cobwebs outside. I mop out the dresser and put my books in the top drawer. Then I unpack my clothes. Two pairs of overalls from the Salvation Army tag sale, my black dress, pocket T-shirts in assorted colors, and my most prized collection other than my books: my socks. Most were purchased at thrift stores: Christmas socks, purple socks, wool socks, socks with lace. Church thrift shops were especially good for hand-knit socks, and sometimes after paying a dollar or two for a pair, I would wander upstairs and sit in a pew and wonder what all the fuss was about.

The smell I liked a lot. Incense, heavy and thick, hung like blankets all around me. Me and the statues, surrounded by silence. I liked that the best.

"What the hell you want with church?" my mother said once after I'd told her where I'd been. "You really are a ninny sometimes, Corns. There ain't no one who goes to church but hypocrites and fools. Don't you know that?"

Well, I didn't want to be a hypocrite or a fool, so I shut the door to that part of my life and didn't go back.

Agatha and I climb the rise behind her
house to where the fields begin. The grass under
my feet grows brown and dry and uncut. I crunch through
one pasture, then another, each one rising higher than the last.

Agatha searches for mushrooms, but not me—I won't
have anything to do with them. I just want to get closer to
the mountain that reaches high in the distance. I tell myself
I'm getting closer to my mother with each step.

We turn a bend and there's a brook ahead. She takes a
metal cup off a nail on a tree and climbs down a bank and
scoops up some water. She takes a long, slurping gulp.

"Come taste some of this water. It's the best you'll ever
drink."

I'm not so sure. She eyes me carefully. "This is the real
thing. You've been planted in the city too long."

I sip the water at first, but it fills my mouth with so much
life that I gulp more.

"Where'd you be gettin' that stutter?" she asks as I hand
the cup back to her.

*Why does everyone always ask that? I don't know when. In first grade, I already hated talking, that's all I know.*

I shrug, but I don't know if she sees me, because I'm drinking more water.

We watch two squirrels scream at each other in a pine tree and then we climb over a stone wall and down a short slope and then up another rise. I brace myself for the advice everyone gives, especially my mother: *Try harder, Corns, for goodness' sake. I know you could talk regular if you pull yourself together. Just pick easier words.*

Or the fifth-grade teacher, helpful as hail: *Take a breath, Cornelia. Slow down, relax, think about what you want to say before you say it. You just need more backbone, that's all.*

They made it sound so easy. Try harder, stutter less. But when I try harder, I stutter more. When I pick easier words, I stutter on easier words. And I can't pick an easier word when someone asks me my name.

So I quit talking most of the time. Always better to keep stuff inside. Squish the shame down to your toes if you have to. Keep it hidden there. No one gets it anyway.

# 20

I feel Agatha behind me as I pour suds into her kitchen sink and pile my socks beneath the running water. A rusted washing machine sits unused in the corner of the kitchen, its top spread with clay pots of apple mint and rosemary and sage.

Agatha wears the same overalls day after day and switches from a flannel shirt to a T-shirt, depending on the weather. The only exception she makes to her laundry system is her underclothes. She wears cotton things she calls underdrawers edged in lace and she washes these by hand with soap flakes. Then she hangs them on the branches of an oak near the house, a spot anyone could see from the road.

I fix all this, of course. I hang a clothesline out back, first of all, and get her underwear out of sight.

There isn't much I can do about ironing because she threw her iron away when it broke years ago. "Ironin' makes no sense at all," she tells me one day as I try to press a pair of my overalls with my hands. And of course she keeps no starch and no fabric softener. My clothes smell wonderful when I bring them in from the line, all warm from the sun, but soon they pick up the odor of the house, sort of the way a cupboard smells when it hasn't been opened in a while.

"E-e-e-everything around here s-smells old and d-d-dried out." I am folding clothes into neat piles on the table, my nose buried in one of my shirts.

"You want your clothes to smell good?" my aunt says, looking up from the peas she is shelling. "Then go roll around in the hay."

"Yoo-hoo!" Agatha yells to me through my window one morning. I am reading again. There are no books in this house other than what I brought, and I've read everything so many times I'd read a dictionary at this point.

"Cornelia, I need help getting to the dump." Agatha presses her nose against the screen to see into my room. I sink further into my book. "Get out of that bed and come help me."

I roll over, pretending she is a puff of smoke, gone in an instant. "You read too damn much, Cornelia. You're hiding in those books. Now get your butt out here and give me a hand."

When I don't move, she pulls the screen out of the window. "If you don't get out here, I'm coming in there and dragging you out."

# 22

Agatha hands me a straw hat and then walks quickly to the barn. "What's this for?"

"You'll see," she yells over her shoulder.

As soon as she pushes open the wooden doors, the dry smell of crushed hay and the sweet thickness of old manure soar up my nose. The stalls are empty; the floor lumps with wear. A big pile of trash bags heap in one corner. A broken rake, chipped canning jars, and a coil of old rope lie on top.

When I take a couple of steps forward, I notice a thick netting of spiderwebs strung across the beams over my head. Big fawn-colored spiders crawl through the heavy maze. I stop, unable to move, and pull my hat against my head. *Oh my God.*

"That's why we wear hats," Agatha says, chuckling. "I'll back Bertha up, you start piling stuff on."

I don't move. I want to go home.

"What's the matter with you?" Agatha asks. "Barns have spiders. That's the way it is round here."

I am sure I feel something crawling up my leg. "Why

d-don't you vacuum or something?" I scratch the back of my knee with one hand and use the other to hold the hat on my head.

"A barn? Are you kiddin'?" She laughs and walks off to get the truck. She's still chuckling after she backs up the truck and comes around and grabs a garbage bag.

"You don't know much about barns, do you? You need the spiders to get rid of the flies. Maybe your ma made a mistake bringin' you here."

I am sure of it.

# 23

"Time you met my truck, anyway," Agatha says as we load the first of the bags onto the back. "Bertha, this is Cornelia." She laughs, picks up another bag, and throws it on the back. "I got her in 1975 from Eldin up the road, and she's still the best thing I ever bought. She can haul anything: pumpkins, tires, trash. I use her to pull stumps and to haul manure for the garden. Once I used her to help me hoist Esther up a bit, she was slumping so."

I keep one eye on the spiders and think that Esther could use some more hoisting. "Do you n-n-n-name everything around here?"

"When you live alone, you learn who your friends are. And you treat them fine if you want them to stick around."

Bertha is the same faded green as the unripe tomatoes in the garden. The passenger door is tied shut with clothesline. The tailgate has been repaired with wooden rails. Everything on the inside, I see as soon as I open the door, is patched with duct tape.

"No g-g-garbage trucks?" I ask as we roar out of her driveway and onto Route 1.

She laughs. "You don't think anyone would want to pay for something like that around here, do you?"

It isn't really a question, because Agatha snorts after she says it. I turn and look out the window. We pass a dozen fields, empty, bordered by stone walls. The road turns to gravel as we head south; a deer jumps out in front of us. "Whoa, Bertha, don't you hit that doe," Agatha yells as we bounce over deep ruts in the road. I hold on to the seat.

Agatha pulls onto a dirt road with a sign that says TOWN DUMP. HARRISVILLE RESIDENTS ONLY. The road is littered with old washing machines, refrigerators, air conditioners, and dishwashers. Agatha stops in front of a pile of garbage the size of a small mountain.

"Now comes the fun part." She climbs out of the truck and begins heaving the bags out into the sea of trash. "See who can throw the farthest."

All I can think about is how much everything stinks. Seagulls soar over us, squawking and fighting over our bags as they land. I wonder what's in them.

"Well, look at that," she says, pointing out beyond the gulls.

"L-look at what?"

"That pot! I been needin' one that size for a good while now. It's perfect!"

I try and figure out where her finger is pointing. In front of me, alongside hundreds of bags of garbage, sit a cracked plastic lawn table, a blue croquet ball, a baby's high chair, a rug, rolled and tied, and, just a bit to the back, a pot rusted to the color of an orange marigold.

"Cornelia, go get that pot for me."

I look at the pot, then at Agatha. I'd have to walk up and over several dozen garbage bags to get it. "I'm not p-p-p-picking up trash."

"It's a perfectly fine pot. Just walk right over."

"Why don't you just b-b-buy one at the store?"

"And waste this perfectly good one?"

"It's not perfectly good. It's r-r-r-rusted."

"A little cleanin' and it will shine up good as new."

"Well, I'm n-not picking up a dirty old pot that somebody else used. Plus I'm not walking way out there."

Agatha pulls a sugar cube from her pocket and pops it into her mouth. "You don't want anyone to see you picking up trash, is that it?"

"It's st-st-stupid." I feel something crawling on my arm—an ant. I brush it off and swear under my breath.

Agatha stomps over and pulls a ski hat from under the seat. "Here, pull it down low and pretend you're someone you're not."

I look at her, not quite believing. "Oh, shit." I storm out to the trash and begin walking up and over the bags. My foot sinks into one bag and I smell coffee grounds. I reach for the pot, grab it, and sink farther into the garbage. The pot must weigh ten pounds.

"Good," she says, laughing, as I heave it onto the back of the truck. I kick the coffee grounds off my foot and climb inside and wipe my hands on the duct tape. She pulls the shift into gear and we roar off. "Now I have a pot big enough for my mushrooms."

# 24

Agatha's house sits on a hill, surrounded by pines, and a wind blows constant. As the weeks pass and the summer nights heat up, I learn that all that wind means few bugs fly here; mosquitoes haunt more restful spaces.

But then comes the week of no wind, and the heat grows steadily and the humidity spreads out so thick the wet hangs all around me like a morning fog. That's when the mosquitoes fly in the cracks between the stones in the basement and up between the cracks in the floor and down the chimney and through the beetle-sized spaces surrounding the windows. I toss in bed and dream about mosquitoes and hear their shrill hum and I wake in the morning with red welts that make me look like a plucked chicken.

"Why d-d-don't you f-f-f-fix this house?" I scratch at the bites that cross my arms. Agatha fries a batch of mushrooms in her new pot.

"What's the matter with it?" She opens a canning jar of

some sort of green goo and dumps it into another pan on the stove. Three flies buzz around her hand as she stirs.

"H-h-haven't you noticed? The s-s-s-screens have holes. Look at all these bugs."

"Then fix them." She ladles mushrooms onto her plate and spoons some of the green mixture beside them. "Fishin' line in the barn. Rug needles in the sewin' box back of that cupboard there. Make a spiderweb kind of thing. The time you spend readin', you could be fixin' those screens." She puts her plate on the table and sits down.

I look at her plate more closely. *I live with a woman who eats little green snails.*

"They're fiddleheads," she says after a few bites. "Ferns. Want some?"

I shake my head and walk out to the front step to wait for my mother.

# 25

The boyfriend doesn't know about frozen waffles. He doesn't know that when you stack them five high and dust them with cinnamon and powdered sugar, they will get my mother out of bed on a cold afternoon. The boyfriend doesn't know that a cigarette and a cup of coffee calm her when she starts to shake, and he doesn't know that watching *I Love Lucy* reruns gets her to laugh and improves the day immensely.

My mother is *my* fix-up project, not his. My life is predictable, constant, when it is bookended by one fix-up and then another. I buy carrots and cabbage and peas and puree them into soup so she'll eat something other than Ring Dings. I turn off the gas on the stove after she has fallen asleep with the teapot boiling itself empty. And I feel strong in the fixing. That's the thing. I feel strong in the fixing.

"Carrots got to be thinned to three inches apart," Agatha tells me one morning. "You got to pull the ones that are too close. Like this." She kneels in the middle of the garden, picking tiny seedlings out of the dirt and tossing them into a ragged pile on the side.

I look doubtful. "Why d-d-d-don't we leave them where they are? They l-l-look like babies."

"If we don't thin them out, they won't grow any bigger around than my little finger." Each wispy plant she pulls has a thin thread of orange at the bottom. I look at her throwaways and see myself.

I flop onto the ground. Of all the chores I can think of, gardening is worst. I hate the dirt; I hate the smell of the dirt. I want to go inside and read. I want to read something where the mother gets the love part right.

"What's takin' you so long?" Agatha looks up at me. She's got a smudge of dirt across her forehead and another along the length of her nose. Her braid hangs loose.

I turn my back to her and pull a seedling, then another. I

put them into my pocket. When I fill my pocket, I dig a tiny new garden between the rows and replant all the seedlings she's made me pull.

The sun scorches my shoulders red and as the humidity hurries in, the horseflies follow. Relentless bits of wing and sting, three of them circle my head without stopping. Over and over, they dive at my neck, my back, my face.

"This is n-n-n-nuts," I say, standing and shielding my face from the flies. "I quit."

"You can't quit, not if you want to eat."

"I don't w-w-want to eat carrots. I hate carrots. I hate this. All of it."

I stand there glaring at her while a horsefly lands on my shoulder. She gets up off her knees.

"You're just like your mother," she says. "Temper like a tornado. I didn't ask you to come here, you know." An inch of dirt cakes the knees of her overalls. She doesn't bother to brush it off.

"I didn't ask to c-c-c-come here either," I scream.

"Well, we see eye to eye on one thing, anyway. Now pull those carrots."

"I'm d-done." I wipe my hands on my pants.

"No, you got to finish this row. I'm goin' to clean the hen-house. If you want to eat, you damn well better work."

"H-h-h-horseshit!"

She laughs at me low and hard. "You goin' to cuss, you got to make your voice like you mean it. And it's hen shit I'm cleanin', not horseshit."

Is this the reason I was born? I wonder as Agatha walks off

across the yard. To be dumped off and brought here to this old woman who drinks tea made of tree roots? Let her just think I'm staying here one second past the moment my mother arrives.

"I'm leaving soon as my m–m–m–mother gets here," I yell at her back.

She turns. "I don't see her comin', do you?"

# 27

The next day Agatha slaps a postcard on the table with a picture of a seagull in flight.

I flip it over, afraid to breathe.

> Corns,
>
> No work yet. How's it going with Agatha?
>
> L.

I notice right off there's no *Dear Cornelia,* no *Love, Mother,* and no return address. I wonder if my mother saw her reflection in the glossy front of the card. I throw it in the trash. Then I pull it out and put it in my pocket and walk out to the garden. My carrot seedlings that I replanted lie withered on the ground. I try to stand them up again by mounding their feet in little hills of dirt.

"Don't you know you can't be replantin' carrots?" Agatha says as she walks up from behind. "Their roots ain't strong enough to go down deep."

My fingers scratch themselves raw on a Brillo pad as I bear down harder on the kitchen table. Agatha forgot to wash her molasses spoon, to the delight of the flies. She is so irritating I could spit on her. I push harder and turn the table into a field of steel-blue suds.

Bertha chugs up the driveway and as Agatha slams the door of the truck, she screeches, "Cornelia! Look!"

She rushes into the kitchen and grabs my wet arm, pulling me out the door and into the yard. White fluff swirls all around me.

"I bet you never saw anything like this!" she says. "I'll give you three guesses what it is, and it's *not* snow!" She holds up her fingers and catches the cotton wisps that drift past. I walk out into the middle of the lawn and look straight into the white softness. The fluff looks like large airy snowflakes. I reach for one and hold it in the palm of my hand. "M-m-milkweed?" We raised monarch butterflies in science once.

"No," she says, laughing and spinning around and around. Her braid unropes itself from its pins and flies behind her. "They're dandelions. They're sending off their seed, becomin' something new. This is a lucky day, Cornelia."

She leaps into the air, reaching high for the fluff sailing past, catches some, and tosses it out again. The flour white softens everything and begins to smudge the wrinkles on her face. She springs higher and higher as the wind picks up and sends the wisps heavenward. Even I can't help but smile.

I walk deeper into the gentle flurry. Very slowly, I begin to twirl around, first one way and then the other. I raise my arms, reaching up and pulling pieces of fluff into my hands. I breathe deeply and twirl faster, faster, and as I'm twirling, I'm laughing.

For just a moment, I want to rush into the house and fling on my black Salvation Army dress and dance back through the white softness. And I wouldn't give a hoot about the meanness of anything.

29

"You can eat them, you know," my aunt says that night as she peels a potato at the kitchen table. "Dandelions, I mean."

"The fluff?"

"No," she says, laughing so hard she has to put the potato down. "You really aren't from around here, are you? You eat the leaves. Sauté them up with garlic, toss them in a salad. Either way, they're out of this world."

"Y-y-you'd eat anything, wouldn't you?"

She picks up her potato again and starts peeling.

"You get hungry enough, you eat just about anything. Except for coffee. Rot your stomach out, that will."

# 30

The temperature soars and my aunt and I begin fighting over the chores, the food, the mess, my reading, the lack of coffee in the house. We slam doors and storm outside. She snaps at my cleaning; I yell at her mess. We fume at each other like two chickens in the same sweltering roost.

I wipe the sweat off my forehead and sweep the cobwebs off the beams overhead. I wash down the walls, and while I'm at it, I try to make sense of my life. There is no music in this house, other than the birds outside; no radio, no television. I have nothing to distract me. What now, what now, what now? I ask over and over as I wash the refrigerator, sweep the floor, scrub the stairs, wash the windows.

I slam the cupboard door and run outside when I find little brown pellets at the back of the cupboard.

Agatha kneels beside her squash plants, checking for bugs.

"There's m-m-m-mouse poop in there," I say when I reach her.

She looks up at me. "Set some traps."

"I c-c-can't believe you live in such a m-m-m-mess," I yell, kicking the pumpkin plant in the row next to her, tearing half of it out of the ground. I run up to the fields above the house, sinking into the grass that now reaches to my thighs, screaming until my head aches. All I want is a life that is tidy, where the edges are hemmed and straight and the corners are tucked and tight as new cotton sheets.

# 31

Agatha whacks her moccasins against the side of the fireplace when I walk back into the house. Caked mud flies off the old leather and onto the floor. She ignores the dirt and walks into her room and tosses the moccasins on her bed.

She hasn't touched the mouse droppings, so I take everything out of the cupboards, including old tins of spices with chipped paint hanging off their faces. I sweep out the cupboards, and then I sprinkle an entire can of tub cleaner inside and scrub the wood until it bleaches to a soft buff.

I find mousetraps in the only closet in the house—a little sliver of a thing beside the back door—and I load them with peanut butter and set them behind the plates.

"What you doin' with that there rat trap?" Agatha asks, walking out of her room. "You'll have guts all over the place if you use that. It'll take a mouse head off faster than an ax whacks a chicken. That's for the rats that get into the grain in the barn. What you doin' in that closet, anyway?"

"I was cleaning it s-s-s-so I could p-p-p-put the big soup pot in there. I f-found these."

"Well, top of the stove works just as well for the soup pot. I don't put nothing in that closet 'cept for traps and tools. That crack that's in the back of it goes clear to the outdoors. You can see the stars at night from in there if you look up. It's kind of fun. You should try it sometime."

She pulls a sugar cube from her pocket and munches it slowly. She no longer offers them to me.

"You gotta get used to livin' in a house like this, Cornelia. Why don't you stop wastin' your time and come help me in the garden?"

"If I'm going to l-l-l-live here, I've got to clean it up. How can you live like this?"

She chuckles. "Don't look at it. That works pretty good," she says, walking back outside.

I kick a chair when she leaves. Then I make my way down to the basement. Dozens of jars of home-canned food cover one sloping shelf, but I can't tell what's inside until I wipe the dust with my shirt. Old stringy pickles float in some of the jars, carrots or something orange fills others, and some are stuffed with something that could be beets. Green goo fills a couple dozen jars on the shelf above. I toss them all into old bushel baskets and carry them out to the barn.

# 32

Bertha is loaded with a fifty-pound bag of oatmeal, a twenty-five-pound bag of whole wheat flour, and another of brown rice. We tuck tofu between us on the front seat, lentils on the floor, and dry milk powder in the crawl space behind our seats. Agatha fit right in at the health-food store; I was the only one not wearing moccasins.

"Don't you eat any meat at all?"

"Not for a long while," she says, loading a bag of carob chips. "Doesn't make much sense to me, stuffing myself with dead animals."

The store is in Dover, two towns away, and as we drive back to Agatha's, we pass a bank, a bookstore, a whole string of little shops selling ice cream and antiques and doughnuts.

"C-c-c-can you get me a c-c-coffee?"

"Nah," Agatha says, pulling a thermos from under the seat. "I brought the sassafras."

## 33

**We drive in the slow lane, like we do every-
thing else.** As we head off the highway and into
Harrisville, Agatha pulls Bertha over to the side of the road.
Two wicker chairs sit near a mailbox with a FREE sign hooked
to their backs.

"Well, I can see those out by the barn, can't you?"

No, I can't, I think as she stops. They are the same tomato
green as the truck and are covered with mud. "They don't
even stand up right."

Agatha doesn't listen. She climbs onto the back of the
truck and pushes the oatmeal out of the way. "Are you going
to help me or not?"

As we get the second chair onto the truck, a pickup rum-
bles to a stop. "Agatha!" A man jumps out and hurries toward
us. My aunt plants her feet into the gravel.

"You ladies need a hand?"

"You stop just to give me help, Moss?" Agatha says.

The man laughs. "Sure."

"Well, the job's already done. Two chairs for my garden."

"I did want to talk to you about that woodlot, Agatha. You gonna sell it to me this year?"

She snorts. "I knew there was more. I got the same answer I gave you last year, Moss. No."

"You can make a good pocket of cash off it—I keep telling you that, Agatha."

"And I keep telling you, I'm not lettin' no one buy my land."

He takes off his cap and wipes his forehead with his arm. "Your house, Agatha, it could surely use a little money put into it. Be a shame to let an old place like that go."

"My business, not yours," she says.

He winks at me. "I'm Moss, Moss Jackson." He reaches his hand out to shake mine. "I own the land right up to Agatha's. Isn't that right, Agatha?" He looks back at me. "And you're?"

Think about *anything* else, I tell myself as I reach out my hand. I turn to Agatha, hoping she'll tell him who I am. Instead, she looks back at me. I begin turning myself to stone.

Think about all the fish heads and old bologna sandwiches and half-eaten Pop-Tarts that rot inside all the garbage bags at the dump, I tell myself. Think about tuna in a lunch box, six days old.

"Ummm," I say finally. I breathe deeply through my nose. I loop my thumbs in my belt loops and pull until they are as red as cherries. "C–c–c–c . . ."

A grin moves across his face. He chuckles. "Cat got your tongue?" I turn miserably to Agatha. She is not chuckling. She is looking straight at me.

Why doesn't she do anything? She could just say my

60

name, make this all go away, but she stands there, still as pond water.

I am a stone, sinking. "C–c–c–c–c . . ."

He looks down, away. He turns to Agatha. "You change your mind on that woodlot, you give me a call now, you hear?" He hurries to his truck and climbs in, starts it, and drives off.

Agatha looks at me a long time. She puts her arm on my shoulders and then we walk to the truck and ride home in silence. I want to slip into the quiet and never talk again.

# 34

"You c-c-c-could have helped me," I say later, after we push the chairs off the truck and shove them against the barn, where they sit in the shade of the maple tree. Agatha flips a cucumber basket upside down and sprawls in one of the chairs and puts her feet up. She raises an eyebrow. "How?"

"You c-could have said my name. S-s-something."

"Seems like no one should be doin' that but you."

I turn away and storm into the house.

## 35

Agatha sleeps under a heap of sheets and blankets, with her feet sticking out the bottom of her bed. The whole thing drives me crazy and one day I tackle her room. I strip the bed and wash the sheets and blankets and hang them on the line. I wash her overalls and T-shirts that are strewn over chairs and across the bedposts and are stuffed behind the door. The dust chokes me as I yank things out from under her bed. It's an archaeological dig: I pull out a stuffed owl with one eye missing, yellowed newspapers from 1961, a purple hat with a long sweeping feather, and a small wooden box with a hinged cover.

I brush off her bed with my hand and sit down and open the cover of the box and find the tiniest sweater I've ever seen, a pair of booties, mittens the size of strawberries, and a hat that could fit an orange. A thin thread of lace edges the sweater and when I rub it against my cheek, the yarn feels as soft as the dandelion fluff in the yard.

"What are you doing?" Agatha's voice claws at me; her eyes are nickels on fire. In one leap she hovers over me, pulling the sweater out of my hand. "I ain't never told you to clean in here. Now get out."

I run out to a tree in the backyard where the branches start low enough to climb. From up high, I can look across the backyard to the fields. A bird struggles to put branches into a tiny hole in the birdhouse by the garden. The branches stretch longer than the bird, but she keeps trying to push the sticks through the hole, first one way, then the other, trying to make a home in a place that doesn't fit.

## 36

Not one car passes by Agatha's house in half a morning. My mother must have known what she was doing, leaving me at a house three miles from the center of town, a place with no train tracks, no buses, no taxis, and no easy way out. I look up at the mountain in the distance.

A picture of fried eggs and sausages covers the front of my mother's next postcard. A bright neon light spells out the words *Lou's Diner*.

> Corns,
>    I got a job here. Joe is looking for work.
>                                          L.

Her handwriting is quick and sloping. I can tell she has other things to do.

# 37

"Can I help you with something?"

The voice behind the desk at the library fills me like warm milk. I shake my head, smile, and walk to a back wall. I want fiction, a book to get lost in, a book where the mother comes back for the daughter.

"There's a shelf over there you might like to look at for school." Warm Milk smiles.

I walk over and find several dozen books on the summer reading list at the high school. There's a separate stack of honors books. *To Kill a Mockingbird* sits on the tenth-grade shelf and I pull it down and walk over to a sofa upholstered in a material covered with books.

"Excuse me?" Warm Milk taps at my shoulder. "We're closing now. Would you like to take that with you?"

I jump a little, surprised that a dusky sky now hangs outside the window.

"It's after eight. You can take that home, you know," she says, smiling again.

I don't have a library card. To get one, I'd have to tell her my name.

I shake my head and swallow my voice and leave the book on the table. I am a flower folding into myself, my petals wrapped up tight.

# 38

A truck sputters up behind me.

"Get in," says my aunt.

We're still not talking to each other, but I am glad she came looking for me before it got too dark, so I grab on to the strap that hangs from the ceiling and climb inside as we begin bouncing along the road that the boyfriend drove me in on. We bounce over potholes and a tree limb that has fallen across the road. We bounce past the stone soldiers on the town common and past the general store, now empty. We do it all without talking.

Agatha slows at the driveway, then turns up, scraping the sides of the truck on some bushes before bouncing to a stop. She pulls a sugar cube from her pocket and tosses it into her mouth.

"I seen a moth this mornin', Cornelia, brown and ragged as a dead leaf on the ground," she says, crunching on the sugar cube.

La-dee-da-dee-da, I think as I look straight ahead and she turns the key. The truck backfires, not wanting to turn off.

"Most of the time it kept its wings closed tight as a young head of cabbage. But now and again, it'd fan them wings open and it'd show me what it kept hidden inside. It was a stained-glass window in there, all reds and oranges and yellows. What a sight, beautiful as the sun coming up. But most of the time it kept them wings shut up tight. Looked like a walkin' paper bag."

I wonder what's coming next.

Agatha looks up at the stars that are poking through the sky. "You're all mad and crusty on the outside, Cornelia."

I climb out of the truck, slamming the door, then storm along the walk and into the house. "Y-y-you don't know anything about anything," I yell at the moccasins I hear padding behind me.

I hurry into my bedroom and stuff my head under my pillow and think about how much I really want that library book.

# 39

*Whamwhamwhamwham.*

I wake pretty fast when someone kicks at the front door.
Even without coffee, I'm unfolding myself from the crescent
shape I've crunched into all night on the little bed. Where's
Agatha?

Out the window I see a young girl standing on the front
step, looking up at me through bangs that hang in long sticky
strings. She's wearing thick work boots several sizes too big,
the long laces wrapped round and round at the top near her
shins. She holds a box covered with a faded towel.

"The Crow Lady, is she here?" the girl asks when I open
the door. She looks behind her, then back at me.

I don't know who she means. "Who?"

"The lady that lives here. Is she here?"

*You mean Agatha? I've been left with a woman people call the
Crow Lady?*

"My mother made this for her." The girl hands the box to
me. She looks behind her again. I take the box and look under

the towel, where two loaves of homemade bread lie nested close.

"My ma is thankin' the Crow Lady for the potatoes." The girl hands me a letter. "You're not scared of her or nothing?"

I'm not sure what to say to that, so I just stare at the bread. *The Crow Lady?*

"Lots of kids hold their breath when they walk past here. They say she's loony." The girl pushes her bangs away from her face. "But I don't think so. She brings us stuff."

The girl looks out at the road. "I been here too long. My pa will whip me real bad if he knows I'm here. My ma has to sneak sometimes." She turns to go. "Don't tell nobody it was me that brought it. You won't, will you?"

"I d-d-d-d-don't even kn-kn-kn-know who you are."

She looks at me for several seconds. "Don't say nothing. My pa's gonna beat my tail if you tell."

She turns and runs down the steps and off toward the road.

# 40

I leave the bread on the table for Agatha.

"Where'd this come from?" she asks a few hours later as she lugs a bag of groceries into the room and sets it on the table. She's wearing the hat.

"A l-l-l-little girl."

I look through the grocery bag. There's flour and sugar cubes and milk and organic peanut butter, but no coffee.

I hand her the letter. She brushes it away.

"Read it for me," she says, walking over to the counter for a knife. "I need glasses."

I shake my head.

"You read all the damn time," Agatha says, her voice sharp. "You read too much, if you ask me. Now I need a hand."

The hell I will. Reading to myself isn't the same as reading out loud. She knows that much by now.

She slices a two-inch chunk off the loaf, slathers it with molasses, and takes a bite. "I think it's time I get something out of you readin' so damn much. I can't pay for no glasses right now."

The knot in my throat tightens. I never know which feels worse, the anticipation of reading aloud or the shame when I do. I glare at Agatha.

She cuts another slice and pops it into her mouth. I look up at the mountain. If I leave now, how will my mother find me? I grab the note, pick it up. " 'Th-th-th-th . . .' " I stop, gulp some air. " 'Thank you for the p-p-p-potatoes. I don't kn-kn-know how we would have gotten through the w-w-w-win-ter. L-l-l-lydia.' " I throw the note on the table.

"Lydia always did make the best bread." Agatha leaves the loaves on the counter and walks across the kitchen and out the back door.

# 41

"Where's my fiddleheads?" Agatha yells at me one morning. "All my jars down in the cellar. They ain't there!"

I roll over in bed, tuck my head under the pillow to block her out. "Who told you to clean down there? Cornelia, get up!"

I sit up. "Those d-d-d-disgusting old jars? I threw them in the barrel in the barn."

Her eyes spark. "You threw them away? Do you know how much work it is to get enough fiddleheads? You can only get them for a couple of weeks in the spring and you have to go down the bank by the brook and it takes hours and hours and hours to get a few jars. Who told you to throw them away?"

She storms out of my room. With my window open, I hear her swearing at me as she storms out to the barn.

That afternoon, a dozen jars of fiddleheads fill the cupboard over the stove.

"You didn't break 'em all" is about the only thing she says to me for the next few days.

# 42

I've had enough. I stuff my books and my socks and my mother's postcards into my suitcase and pack as many clothes as I can fit.

Agatha is checking on her woodlot across the road, making sure Moss isn't cutting down there. I open the screen door and a screw near the top pops loose and the door slumps lopsided from its bottom hinge. I shove it back into place and use the front door.

I look back at the mountain, considering it, but I'm not sure if I could make it all the way up and over, and I'm not sure that it would get me to Vegas, anyway, so I push that dream out of my head and walk to the road.

## 43

Cornfields stretch out as far as I can see. Red-winged blackbirds scold me as I pass a grassy brook, and a bobolink flies to the telephone wire that strings from pole to pole to my right. Agatha has taught me a lot about birds, I think as I watch the bobolink watch me in his tuxedo of black and white.

I get about five miles out of town when I can't carry the suitcase anymore and a blister splits the skin on my third toe. I step into a little ditch, climb on a stone wall, pull off my sneaker, and wonder what I'm going to do.

After a while, I snap open my suitcase and take out my mother's postcard, the one with Lou's Diner on the front. I don't know much about Vegas except that it is someplace in Nevada and it's hot and it's dry and it's about as far away from New England as you can get. I wonder if there are any bluebirds or barn swallows or barred owls that call "Who cooks for you? Who cooks for you?" in the middle of the night the way they do at Agatha's. There probably aren't any stone walls there, I think, settling down on the one I'm sitting on.

But I want my mother. She made a mistake bringing me here; that's as plain as Wonder Bread. I had planned on walking until I got to a bus station. Where I come from, there's a bus at every corner, but I have gone miles now and there's nothing but this road.

I am chomping on an apple when I hear the low-pitched grinding of Bertha's engine. Agatha has turned her headlights on, even though it's early, and the light on the right tilts toward the sun. She sees me just as I am finishing my apple. Bertha backfires, refusing to turn off. Agatha climbs out of the truck, slamming the door behind her, then walks over to where I'm sitting, pulling a sugar cube from her pocket and popping it into her mouth. She is so blasted irritating, I think, watching her.

"What you doing down there, Cornelia? That ditch is filled with all kinds of stuff you don't like, I bet."

I rub my toe.

She walks over to the edge of my suitcase. "See this little hummock here?" She bends down and inspects a clump of weedy grass. "Now, if this was more of a brook, not just standing water full of mosquitoes, we might have some fiddleheads growing here. They do like gravel like this, yes, they do."

I roll my eyes.

Agatha sits down on a large rock. Bertha smells as if Agatha ran over a load of manure a while back. I swat a mosquito off my arm.

"Cornelia, you ain't never goin' to find your mother this way."

I shrug, look bored.

"Does she tell people who you are when you don't do it yourself?"

I look the other way.

"She does or she doesn't, it don't matter. I'm not goin' to do it."

I ignore her, put my sneaker back on. My toe hurts something awful. She takes the last of the apple out of my hand and chomps on it. "You don't do your own talkin', you're going to be sorry someday."

"D-d-d-don't worry about me," I say.

She stands and throws the core into the corn. "You hide who you are, you live half a life. You speak up, then you can be who you was meant to be."

My eyes become two fat blazing suns. I jump up and face her, hobbling a bit. Tall as she is, I reach her chin. "And j-j-just who the *hell* is that?"

She looks straight back at me. "That's why you got two feet, Cornelia: to put one in front of the other to find out."

"That's wh-what I'm doing, see?" I pick up my suitcase and limp away from her.

"But you're going the wrong way."

I turn around. "How do *you* know the right way?" I yell at her. "You d-d-don't know *jack shit* about anything, far as I can tell."

She looks away for an instant, then straight back at me. "I know it's easy to get all mixed up when you try and do it alone."

# 44

Later that night I come out to the kitchen, looking for a new Band-Aid for my toe. Agatha is sitting at the table, holding the tiny sweater.

"You think I don't know what it feels like to be alone, Cornelia?" She doesn't look up. Her voice is low, hard. "Felt every winter blow right through this old house for forty years, all alone ever since my baby died.

"I know plenty about standin' alone, Cornelia. I know about havin' a husband and I know about havin' that husband run off before our baby cut her teeth because he couldn't take havin' a baby that wasn't right in the head. I know about doctors who told me a woman all by herself couldn't take care of a baby as sick as that and I know about letting them put her in one of those hospitals. She died there."

She pushes the sweater in front of me. I look at the soft woolen stitches that hook together in tiny, orderly twists and I think that I may not know much about losing a husband or about having a baby die, but I know *a lot* about being dumped off by your mother.

80

"In a hospital? You mean for good? You left her there?"

She looks at me, furious, then picks up the sweater and storms into her bedroom and slams the door.

# 45

A few days later, I hear the whacks of Agatha's ax in the woods not far from my bedroom window. Then I watch her drag a young tree to a spot near the barn and chop off the branches and peel off the bark. This takes until nearly lunchtime. She leans the trunk of the tree against the barn. Without its leaves and branches, it is a long thin pole.

The next afternoon, Agatha pulls two more trees from the woods and chops off their branches and strips their bark. The outhouse shakes a bit when I close the door lately and I wonder if Agatha plans on using them to prop up old Esther, but when she finishes, she drags the poles to the barn, right past our own Leaning Tower of Pisa.

I sigh and put the outhouse on my list of things to tend to and sink my hands into the dishwater and finish the breakfast dishes.

I don't ask her what she has been up to when she comes in for supper, but I notice that she has pulled another tree from the woods and left it stripped of its bark in front of the barn. Like a fly intent on a piece of watermelon, I can't stop thinking about it.

# 46

A jeep drives up with lights flashing and stops at the mailbox as I walk across the yard. A man reaches out and pushes a couple of letters into the folds of Agatha's smashed metal mailbox. When he sees me, he motions for me to come over.

"How come the old lady never fixes this mailbox?" He chomps down on his cigar and hunts through the box on the seat beside him.

He points to the house. "I've seen you around here a few times. You a relative of hers?"

I nod.

"Well," he continues, "there's rules about how to keep your mailbox, you know. Tell her."

He hands me an armload of mail. "Everything's gonna get all wet if she doesn't do something about this." He shakes his head, puts the jeep into gear, and drives off.

When I walk into the kitchen, Agatha is sorting through dried lentils, pulling out bits of stone.

"Throw it in that bucket over there," she says, looking up.

"Where?" I look around. "You mean the trash?"

"No, by the stove. Now hurry and put these beans on. If we don't get them on, we won't be having supper."

"But there m-m-m-might be something in here you need." I look at the flyer. There's a sale on coffee at the A&P.

"Don't think so." She pulls a tiny stone out of the lentils and drops it in a cup.

"But there may be bills or s-s-s-something."

She looks up at me, exasperated. "Bills come the first of the month. When there's a need to pay them, I do."

I sift through the rest of the pile. There's nothing from my mother.

# 47

"You can't go to t-t-t-town like that," I snap as Agatha climbs into the truck.

She has topped off her usual attire of overalls and moccasins with the purple hat. She ignores me. The cracked seat in the truck bakes in the heat, and as we drive off and along the road into the next town, it just gets hotter. By the time we climb out of the truck and walk along the sidewalk to the bank, my throat feels as hot as the street.

"I d-d-d-don't see why you just don't write those checks at home and send off the bills like everyone else. Then we wouldn't have to be out here in all this heat."

"Always done it this way," she grumbles as she crosses the parking lot. Her moccasins scuff quietly along the hot pavement.

A long line of customers loops around a course set by velvet cords inside the bank. An older man in black-rimmed glasses considers Agatha intently as her feather flies in the breeze of an oversized fan on the floor. When she realizes he's staring at her, she looks up and he looks down at his watch.

Agatha shuffles through her bills as she waits. She doesn't read them; she just fans through them with her hands.

I wait behind. I pick up a bank newsletter from a stack on a table and back up a few paces and bump into a man in a flannel shirt with the arms cut short.

Papers fly out of his hand. "I'm s-s-s . . ." I stop and bend down and pick up a check that has fluttered to the floor and hand it to him.

"Watch what you're doing," he says, pulling his check from my hand.

"I'm s-s-s . . . ," I try again.

He looks up from his bills. "What's the matter with you?"

I take a breath and blow it out. "I'm s-s-s-sorry." I look at the floor.

He shakes his head and walks into the line.

"Next!" the bank clerk says, and Agatha walks to the window. She turns and motions for me to join her. I watch her feather swing as I make my way to the front of the line without looking at the man in the flannel shirt.

"I need your help readin' these," she whispers. "I ain't got glasses."

Agatha lays the oil bill, the tax bill, the telephone bill, and the electric bill on the counter and places four blank checks beside them.

"Sure is hot out there, isn't it, Agatha?" the clerk says as she picks up the blank checks and rolls them into her typewriter.

Agatha nods.

The clerk begins typing, and when she finishes, she hands the typed checks back to Agatha.

"You can sign all of these, Mrs. Thornhill. But there's not enough in the account for this one."

"I'll be skippin' that one for another month, then, Betty." Agatha stuffs the telephone bill into the pocket of her overalls.

Agatha nods to the man in the flannel shirt as we walk past while I look at my feet. "Pete," she says. He grumbles something that I can't make out.

"This is a t-terrible amount of work, coming here like this to write bills," I complain again as we walk out into the heat, despairing that my mother won't be able to call me for another month.

"Always is." Agatha climbs into the truck and starts the engine. I open the door and climb in beside her. "That's why," she says, "I was tellin' you I only do it once a month."

## 48

"I could use some ice cream," Agatha says as we back out of the parking space.

She pulls out into traffic and drives about a mile before stopping in front of Hal's Ice Cream.

A long line of mothers and fathers and children stands waiting for takeout. One father in front of us pulls a toddler up into his arms while another child sends a toy truck roaring along the floor.

I stare at the menu hanging on the wall to keep my mind off the waitress, who rushes through her customers. "What can I get you?" she asks when it is our turn. She eyes Agatha's hat and feather.

"Let's see," says Agatha. "Do you want to order first, Cornelia?" I shake my head quickly and begin turning myself to stone.

"All right, then." Agatha looks over to see what a young couple is eating. The waitress taps her pencil against her order pad. "Yes, that's it," Agatha says finally. "I'll have a hot fudge sundae with strawberry ice cream, whipped cream, and nuts.

Extra nuts. A large sundae. Extra large." Agatha chuckles and her feather bobs.

"What will you have?" The waitress has turned to me.

I turn to Agatha. "Order for m-m-m-me," I whisper.

"No," she says in a voice three times as loud as mine. "You got to make your own way." She rustles through her overall pockets, looking for money.

"I don't care who orders, but somebody's got to." The waitress looks up at the clock.

I take a deep breath.

"C-c-c-c-o . . ." The waitress sighs and taps her pencil. I push my foot into the floor, trying to force the sounds out. "C-c-c-c . . ." Then I look at the floor.

"Well, make up your mind—I haven't got all day, you know." The waitress looks away.

"C-c-c-o . . ." I stop again.

"Chocolate?" She taps her pencil faster. "Is that what you're trying to say? Chocolate?"

I shake my head miserably. I look up at Agatha. She looks straight at me.

"No. Not ch-ch-ch . . ." The waitress looks at a woman beside us and rolls her eyes.

"Is there something the matter with you?" the waitress asks.

I fold into myself. Where's my mother? I look for her in the crowd.

"Can you please order for this girl?" the waitress asks Agatha.

Agatha shakes her head.

"Strawberry," I say in a voice so quiet I can hardly hear myself.

"Is this some kind of a joke?" the waitress snaps. "Don't think I don't have enough to do," she says loud enough for nearly everyone else to hear—and everyone does, I'm sure, because they are staring at me.

In a moment the waitress hands Agatha a sundae the size of a skyscraper. I lick my cone slowly because I hate strawberry ice cream.

# 49

At home Agatha carefully signs her checks. She writes like a child, in slow, wobbly handwriting. Then she puts a stamp on each envelope and carries them out to the mailbox.

## 50

The little girl comes back with another loaf of bread one day, and then, as the beans begin to ripen, she shows up every day and goes straight to the garden, where she helps Agatha pick. Most days she carries a bag filled with green beans and wax beans and zucchini and lettuce and parsley home with her.

They laugh when they garden together. I can hardly believe the girl stays out there so long. When they finish one day, they head for the woods and a while later the girl and Agatha drag another tree into the backyard.

I'm hanging out laundry one day when the girl walks up behind me.

"Have you ever seen one so big?" She laughs delightedly as she holds out a frog the size of one of her boots.

Its bulging eyes look at me without blinking. Its legs hang down, its webbed feet spread.

"Ugh," I say, holding a towel in front of me.

"Oh, don't worry none," she says, giggling. "He won't

hurt you." She puts the frog into a canvas bag. "There's a race at the school on Friday. I catched this big guy in the creek across the road. Want to come race him?"

Naaaaah, I think. I shake my head and hang up Agatha's purple T-shirt.

"How come you never talk to the Crow Lady and me or nothing?" She buckles the flap of the bag over the frog. I shrug and hang up some of Agatha's underwear.

"This is really going to be fun, you know. It's a frog race."

"No th-th-thanks." I reach over and grab a pair of my socks.

"What can be more fun than racin' a frog?"

I hang the socks on the line, toe to the top. "Cl-cl-cl-climbing that m-m-m-m-mountain." I nod to the horizon.

"It's far up there. My pa would kill me if I went." She swings the pack over her shoulders. "I know another mountain that's closer. I'll take you there if you don't tell anyone and if you promise to go to the frog race."

I consider her offer.

"My name's Bo." She holds out her hand. I check it for frog goo.

## 51

"Wh-wh-where's the mountain?" I sputter.

Bo points to a church steeple in the center of town. We have just run most of the three miles here.

"That's no m-m-m-mountain."

"It is so." She laughs.

I stand straight and face her. "I r-r-ran all this way, I was expecting a m-m-m-mountain."

"It is. Don't be mad. We'll see clear to Boston up here."

Bo runs up the stone steps and pushes the front door open and walks inside. I look behind myself and then follow her. I feel like a burglar.

"It's always open," she tells me. "For people to come pray."

We walk into a front hall. Straight ahead, sunlight rushes into the sanctuary through stained glass windows, and a statue of Mary, crowned in roses, watches me. Please don't tell any-one I'm here, I tell her. I don't want to be a hypocrite or a fool.

"There's not much to hold on to up there," Bo says as she reaches up and climbs onto a ladder that runs up against the back wall and through a hole in the ceiling. "Watch out for the nails. And whatever you do, don't touch that rope." A thick rope hangs through the hole and ends in a coil on the floor. "It rings the bell."

Someone's going to come is all I can think. Bo climbs through the hole in the ceiling and disappears. I take my first step and by the time I have crawled through the first hole and see that I am climbing up through the attic of the church, she has climbed through another hole, up another story. Old hymnbooks and robes for the choir, broken chairs, a box of opened paint cans, and a piano stool with its legs hacked off lie on the floor. Having lived with Agatha all these weeks, I know the difference between a mousetrap and a rat trap. Rat traps lie in a heap near a rolled-up carpet. My arm touches a spiderweb as I wrap my fingers around the ladder rungs and climb.

Next I'm inside a narrow space, almost as wide as our outhouse. Rusted nails poke in from the outside. The wood smells tired. I think of a tinderbox and keep climbing.

"You got to keep moving," Bo says. "Else you get scared. That's the trick of the whole thing."

The wood creaks something terrible each time the steeple sways with the wind. I keep looking below me because the creaking sounds as if someone is following.

The steeple rises another story. Bo scurries up through another hole. My legs ache from the climb and my fingers ache from wrapping so tightly around the rungs. Cars whiz past far below. "If you pull that rope, we go deaf," Bo yells down to me.

When I finally pull myself through another hole, I am flooded by light. A bell the size of our kitchen table hangs silent and still above me. Large windows covered with screens light the space. Bo sits on a wide beam below the bell, her feet hanging down into the emptiness.

"Isn't this the greatest place you've ever been?"

I climb up next to her, grabbing on to a beam above me. My legs hang down and my socks catch the sun. The tower sways, and I grab tighter.

"I watched a guy come fix the bell one day. I watched him climb up. Now I come a lot." She laughs. "What's your name, anyway?" she asks. "You never told me."

I pretend I don't hear. I look out the screen closest to me. A newspaper truck dashes past.

"Do you have a name? Of course you do. Everyone has a name. Even the bell has a name. I call him Big Ben. What's yours?"

"Uh-uh-uh." I tap my finger on my leg, trying to concentrate on my taps instead of what I'm going to say. "C-c-c-c-c-cornelia."

"Nice name." Bo looks straight at me. "How come you talk funny sometimes?"

I shrug. Sweat begins to form on the back of my neck.

"I mean, it doesn't sound bad or nothing, just different. Slower or something. I don't mind, though."

"No?"

"No. Everyone's got something. My pa's got a rotten temper. Me, I can't read too good."

"Why not?"

97

"I don't know. I just don't get it. The letters get all mixed up. There's a summer class at the school, but it costs twenty-five dollars and my pa says he's not paying nothing extra to the school."

A group of boys walk past us down below. One bounces a ball. We see them, small as beetles.

"How long is the Crow Lady gonna watch you?"

I shrug. "Until my m-m-m-mother comes back. Why do they call her the C-crow Lady?"

"My ma told me that people say that when she was a little girl, they all got so hungry in that house they ate crows. People get wind of something like that, they never let it go, I guess."

I shrug and tell her Agatha really is kind of a crazy lady and the kids in town probably should hold their breath when they walk past her house. "Why do they do that, anyway?"

"It's silly. It's like not stepping on a crack, something like that. It's really dumb 'cause she's nice to me. And to my ma and the rest of us."

"I've n-n-n-never seen her do anything but w-w-work in the garden. Or chop trees. What's she d-doing with those trees, anyway?"

"I promised I wouldn't tell."

Bo giggles. A tractor-trailer downshifts on the road below. The steeple creaks, a long thin backbone rising to the sky. The bell sways silently above me.

I breathe deeply, look up at the bell. I consider for the first time that maybe my speech might not be so terrible, that my throat may not be so wounded after all, and that I may not be alone.

Another postcard waits for me on the table.
This one has a picture of a desert sun beating down on a
house trailer:

> Corns,
>    Hot as hell here. We moved into this trailer
> park. How you making out in that old house?
>                                            L.

# 53

"I guess I be needin' some glasses right away," Agatha says, looking up at me from her place at the table. "Who's this one from?"

I open the envelope for her. "S-s-s-senior Citizen Center. They want you to b-b-buy a cookbook."

"Don't they know I hate cookin'?"

I smile and let her fix me a cup of sassafras. I'm starting to like the way it fills me.

I'm measuring whole wheat flour into the bread bowl, trying not to put in seven scoops of flour rather than six, when the screen door slams with a bang.

"Corney." Bo hurries into the kitchen, her pants soaked, mud up her arms and across her cheeks. "I need another frog. The race is tomorrow."

"Wh-wh-what happened to the other one?"

"My brother let it go. I been down the creek for an hour, but I can't catch anything. I need you to help me get one." She drops her canvas sack on the floor.

I look up at the clock. If I want this heavy whole wheat flour to rise, I have to knead it for a full ten minutes. I plunge my arms deep into the dough, pushing it down into a pancake, folding it back on itself, and punching it down.

"I n-n-n-never caught a fr-fr-frog before, Bo."

"But with two of us, maybe we could trap one. You promised you'd go to the race with me."

I put the dough into a bowl, spread a towel across the top, and set it on the counter in the sun.

"I know," I say, wiping my hands on a towel. "But I didn't promise I'd c-c-c-catch a frog."

## 55

Over and over, I run through the water toward Bo and watch a frog jump almost close enough for her to catch in her out-stretched arms.

The water is cold. My waterlogged overalls weigh me down, my body a heavy barrel I pull through the water. A frog jumps close to Bo and this time she dives for it. When she stands, black mud from the bottom of the pond covers her face and plasters her hair.

"B-b-b-bo, this isn't working at all." Mosquitoes bite my neck. Each time I swat at them, I leave a muddy handprint behind.

"Maybe not. Let's go around the other side. Come on."

We scramble along the edge of the pond and across the brook where the water enters. Blueberries hang so low at the edge they bob like marbles on the water.

I see a frog close to me this time and I spring, grabbing the air and landing facedown in the mud. When I stand up, Bo laughs.

"Is that the way you do it in the city?" she asks. "Leapfrog? You're not supposed to eat the mud." She laughs so hard I'm sure she's going to pee her pants. I try to wipe my face with my wet sleeve.

A car slows and stops. Bo splashes around the blueberry bushes and doesn't hear. A man walks up to the crest of the hill and looks down at us. I can tell the moment he sees her.

"Bo!"

She looks up at him, her hair hanging in wet strings. "Pa!"

"I never said you could come here," he says, rushing down the bank and wading toward us. "You expect us to do all your work?"

I don't know why he hasn't seen me. I am standing in a shadow; maybe I am a shadow. But when I take a step forward, he jumps. "Who the hell are you?"

I recognize him as soon as he speaks. He's the man from the bank.

"We were just catching frogs, Pa. That's all. I finished all my chores before I came."

He hasn't taken his eyes off me. "Who's this?"

I take a deep breath. "C-c-c-c . . ." Then I stop, unable to go on. I might be standing knee-deep in water, but my face sparks. He reaches for Bo's arm, misses, and wades closer. He looks at me without blinking.

"Who are you?"

"Cor-cor-cor . . ." I stop and start again. "C-c-c-cornelia."

He recognizes me; I can see it in his eyes. Then he looks away.

"Dimwit," he says, half under his breath. He drags Bo out

104

of the water, up the hill, and into the car. I sink to a rock and reach up to wipe the mud from my face.

# 56

I carry a frog into Agatha's kitchen a couple of hours later. It squirms so much I keep tightening my fingers around its slender body. It is half the size of the one Bo caught a few days ago. But it is alive and green. I can attest to the fact that it hops as high as my face.

Agatha looks up from the cucumbers she is slicing.

"What happened to you?"

I tell her the story and drip on the floor.

"Maybe you should race it for her," Agatha says.

"Name, please."

A boy wearing a sign on his chest that says FROG JUMPING COMMISSIONER looks up at me. Behind him, someone has taped a set of rules, written on poster board in thick black paint:

## OFFICIAL RULES

1. No toads.
2. Any frog jockey who is rough will be asked to leave the race.
3. A jump is measured by running a string from the start line to the frog's front feet after it has hopped three times.
4. DO NOT ARGUE WITH THE FROG COMMISSIONER.
   - ALL JUDGMENTS ARE FINAL •

# 58

The frog commissioner looks up at me when I don't answer.

"I said, Name, please."

"Ummmmm." I try to ride the vibrating wave of the *m* sound, hoping I can break into *Cornelia* without blocking on empty air. I look for Bo in the crowd, even though I don't expect to see her. A boy with a frog twice the size of mine edges forward. "What's going on?"

"If you want to race, I need your name," the commissioner says again. "Are you going to race or not?"

I take a deep breath and push my foot into the ground. "C-c-c-c . . ." I stop.

"What?"

More of the kids behind me move closer now. "C-c-c-c-c . . ." I want to sink into the ground.

The commissioner looks at me unbelieving, then laughs. "What's the matter, forget your own name?"

I take another breath and laugh right along with him. Then I spell my name. The easy way out is as simple as *J-e-l-l-O.*

"Jockey, on your mark." A couple dozen kids kneel down around the circumference of the starting circle while I hold my frog in front of me. They're all supposed to keep their frogs under control while I jump mine. This is a one-frog-at-a-time race.

The boy on my left holds a frog with massive legs the size of my entire frog. My frog's legs look like knitting needles.

One kid loses control of his frog and watches it jump crazily out of the circle and across the pavement and the boy screams out, "Stop, stop!" but of course it doesn't listen. I tighten my grip.

"Get ready!" screams the frog commissioner. "Go!"

# 60

Two chained German shepherds growl and bark as I round the corner and walk up Bo's driveway. A woman walks out of the house and wipes her hands on a dish towel and watches me from the porch. Two toddlers grab at her legs, peeking from behind her floured apron. Her stomach sticks out so far with a baby on the way it looks as if she's tucked a laundry basket under her dress.

I glance around quickly for the father. There's no car in the driveway. Several chickens peck at the ground, which is worn thin and bare and hard as an old carpet. A cracked bathtub tilts on the grass, filled with muck.

"Is B-b-b-bo here?"

The mother looks me over. "You Lenore's girl?" Her voice softens. She makes my mother's name sound welcoming, promising, kind.

I nod.

"Bo told me you're at Agatha's. You look just like your mother. Like Agatha, too. Come on in. I've got something for you.

"Bo's out in the back with the boys. I baked this morning." We walk into the kitchen and she pulls a chocolate cake out from beneath a checked towel that sits on the stove and wraps it in tinfoil and hands it to me.

"There's no frosting on it so it won't get all over everything. Would you like a piece? I've got another. Have a seat." She points to a table in the middle of the kitchen that sits on an orange and brown braided rug.

The toddlers peek at me from behind her skirt and she drags them along behind her as she pulls a jelly glass from a cupboard and fills it with milk.

Faded curtains cover the window. An old white sink sits near the stove with a built-in drainboard on the end. The room smells like chocolate.

"All those potatoes. Agatha really helped us over the winter. My husband found a job, so things are better now. You can tell Agatha. And tell her I appreciate the vegetables Bo brings home, I surely do." She smiles and cuts me a slice from the other cake and lays it in front of me.

"How's your mother?"

I shrug.

"She still the same?"

I nod, although I'm not sure if we're talking about the same thing.

"She'll come around. Sometimes it takes a while." She smiles at me again.

I'm not so sure I should have to wait at all. I'm pretty sick of waiting, actually. But instead of saying anything, I take another piece of cake. Bo is lucky to have a mother like this,

I think. They both have the same kindness. I feel the warmth
coming up through me as I take another bite of cake.

## 61

Bo covers her eyes and counts and three little boys dash away from her as I walk around back. A rusted swing set with one swing missing stands near the house.

"I got you a r-r-ribbon," I say, walking up to her. "A yellow one."

"How'd you do that?" She pushes the bangs out of her eyes and turns to the boys. "Don't go too far!"

"I caught a frog in the pond. I won a yellow ribbon."

"Wow, that's so great, Corney. Let me see."

I pull the ribbon out of my overalls pocket and give it to her.

"Wow, I wish I could've seen it. How'd you catch the frog?"

"Took me the rest of the morning." I laugh. "You don't get m-m-m-money for third place, though."

She strokes the ribbon. "That's okay. Was it fun?"

I smile. "Yeah. I n-n-n-never raced a frog before."

We both laugh.

"Want to play with us?"

I shake my head. "I have to go. But if you w-w-want to come over, I can show you some stuff. About r-r-r-r-reading, I mean."

"You mean it? You really do?" When I nod, she jumps up and hugs me and it feels pretty good as I hug her back.

The next day I receive a postcard that sends a storm rushing across the desert.

> Corns,
>    It's not going so well for us here. Joe is out of work again.
>
>                                  Love, L.

Good, I think. She'll be back for my birthday. A mother doesn't forget her daughter's birthday.

# 63

I bring Bo to the library. I scan the shelves, looking for the right book. Finally, I put *Teach Your Child to Read* on the counter. Warm Milk looks up at me and smiles. I look at Bo. "I'd like a library card," she says.

Warm Milk types the card for Bo and hands it to her. "Would you like one, too?"

I shake my head and plant myself facedown again.

"I'll shut the door if you think your p-p-p-pa will come."

Bo slumps at the kitchen table. The heat hangs heavy inside the house and out. The black-eyed Susans droop after an afternoon at the back step. We watch them through the screen door, newly fixed by me, that barricades us against the flies and mosquitoes that followed another bout of humidity.

"Oh, don't worry about him none." Bo laughs and slurps the lemonade I put in front of her. "He's workin' till midnight. He hates it, but our nights are nice and quiet now."

I pull out the phonics book and sit down beside her. "All right, then. If you're sure." I open the book. "We're going to do short v-v-vowel sounds first." I point to a letter *a*. "This makes a sound like the *a* in *apple* or the *a* in *ant*."

Then I show her an *e*. "This m-m-makes a sound like the *e* in *echo* or *egg*."

I point to the *a* again. *"Aa, aa, aa,"* I say. "Now you try."

*"Aa, aa, aa."*

Bo looks at the page intently. Her bangs flop in front of

her eyes and she pushes them away. "How come it doesn't sound like the *a* in *plate*?"

"That's for l-l-l-later." I glance out the door. "Now come on. You have to learn this."

"I just don't get it—why doesn't it sound right?"

There's a bang at the door; we both jump before we realize it's Agatha.

"I got all these tomatoes here," Agatha yells in to us. She dumps the tomatoes into the sink and covers them with water.

"Okay," I say, turning back to Bo, "it just doesn't make s-s-s-sense to ask all these questions. Everyone asks these questions and it gets them nowhere. Now just say after me— *aa, aa, aa.*"

Bo rolls her eyes. *"Aa, aa, aa."*

She turns her face into a sour ball. "I don't want to do *aa, aa, aa,* Corney, I want to read. This is for babies."

"Bo," I say, raising my voice just the tiniest bit, "you have to start at the beginning if you don't want to *be* a baby."

Bo squinches her face and tries again. *"Aa, aa, aa,"* she says softly.

"That's b-b-better. Now for *i,* you make the s-s-sound like in *itch* or *igloo.* Say it—*ih, ih, ih.*"

Bo crosses her eyes at Agatha, who laughs.

"This is so dumb," Bo complains. *"Ih, ih, ih."*

I ignore them.

"Now why don't we p-p-play a game," I say. I tear a piece of paper into four squares and on one square I write the letter *a,* on another an *e,* and on a third an *i.* Then on the fourth square I draw a goose.

"I told you this is for babies," Bo says.

"No, it's going to be fun. Now look. We'll f-f-f-flip these cards over and if you get one of the vowels, you make the sound, but if you get the goose, I make a honking sound and flap my arms like this."

Agatha pulls a tomato out of the sink and begins chopping.

"Okay, pick a card."

Bo picks the goose.

*"Honk, honk, honk, honk,"* I scream. I stand up and run around the table, flapping my arms. *"Honk, honk."*

"Why ain't you teachin' her the words, silly goose?" Agatha says from the counter, chuckling to herself.

"It m-m-makes sense to go slow and make it fun so she can learn it this time," I say, slightly miffed. "I b-b-bet if they made it fun in school, Bo would have learned it the f-f-f-first time around."

Agatha chops a few more tomatoes. "At least she's not too scared to go to school."

I ignore Agatha and turn the page. "We say *o* like *ostrich.*"

Bo interrupts me. "Yeah, Corney, I never knew anyone who reads as good as you. You could go to college."

*College? Me? Do you have to talk in college?*

Agatha interrupts my thoughts. "How long you goin' to hide, Cornelia?"

# 65

Hide? I'm not hiding. I'm waiting for my mother to come back and take me away. I sink my arms deeply into a basket of wet clothes. I grab towel after towel, shirt after shirt, hanging my madness out with wooden clothespins.

"When you goin' to talk about it?" Agatha has walked up behind me. I stiffen but don't turn. Two clothespins jam into my mouth, and I reach down for a pair of my socks.

"You don't talk about your mother, your stutterin', you keep all that inside you, you're goin' to rot like an apple."

I pick up a pair of my socks and add those to the line as she walks away.

She wants me to talk? How? I stuff my feelings and they layer themselves like a parfait dessert in the innermost part of my being.

Inside, where nobody can see, I am glorious with the colors of the girl I wish I could be.

One day a postcard comes with a mother walking hand in hand with a child, and I know, even without flipping the card, that there's been a shift in the barren landscape between my mother and me.

Dear Corns,
  I'm missing you real bad.
                Love, L.

# 67

Something itches at me. It's itched for weeks now, ever since Bo started coming around for reading lessons.

I stand at the counter peeling potatoes and Bo practices her *u* sounds. "'Muck, luck, truck, stuck,'" she reads, her index finger a magnet that pulls her through each word.

But it's not Bo that's making me itch; it's Agatha. She waits at the table every afternoon for Bo. She looks up from whatever bean she's snapping or tomato she's chopping and watches Bo read.

"Corney, I don't know this word," Bo says, looking up from her book. I put my knife down, ready to walk over to her, then pick it up again. The itch runs deep. "Ask Agatha," I say, looking over at my aunt. "I got to get this done."

Agatha looks down to the dried beans she's picking through, hunting for bits of pebble and dirt.

"I'd need glasses for words that small," Agatha says quickly.

I know it's him as soon as the car turns up the driveway. We don't move as he crunches along the gravel to the back door. Even Agatha sits without breathing.

He looks in at us through the screen, his eyes traveling from Agatha to me and then stopping on Bo. "What are you doing here?"

"Pa!" Bo covers the reading book with her hands. Her father unlatches the door without anyone asking him in. Agatha stands. "Pete," she says. I grab hold of Bo's hand.

He ignores us and glares at Bo. "No one said you could come here."

"St-st-stop yelling."

He turns slowly and stares at me.

"This is my niece, Pete," says Agatha. "Now you be calmin' down."

"Calm down? What are you talking about? No one said she could come here. What's going on, anyway?"

His eyes jump from the reading book to Bo's paper and pen to Agatha's beans.

"She's l-l-learning to read," I blurt out, grabbing Bo even tighter.

That fact catches his attention. "Reading? She reads just fine."

When I don't say anything more, he turns to Agatha.

"What is this, you think we need some kind of charity? We don't need it, that's for damn sure." He turns to Bo. "Get out to the car. *Now.*"

I take a deep breath. "She can't r-r-read hardly at all. She c-c-c-c-could never go to college reading like that."

He laughs, sneers. "College? You think I got money to send a *girl* to college?" He grabs Bo's arm and marches her out of my grasp and out the door.

I look at my empty hand, unbelieving. I look up at Agatha, but she is sitting back down at the table, slumping into her arms. I take a deep breath. *What now? What now? What now?* I breathe again and run outside as he crunches toward the driveway. "J-j-just wait," I scream. "She'll go to college. J-just wait."

## 69

"You could hide a book in these potatoes," Agatha says a few nights later, walking up from the cellar.

"How are we g-g-g-going to do that?" I use a towel to wipe whole wheat dough from my hands and walk over to the table.

"Like this." Agatha pulls a dozen potatoes off the top of a bushel basket and lays them on the table. "Put a couple of books in here like this and we'll pile these potatoes back on top." She looks up at me.

"Do you think it could work?"

"Best I can think, it will. Now go get some books."

I pull two books off the counter and hand them to Agatha. "He'll shoot us if he finds out."

"He won't find out. We'll go when he's at work."

When the basket is filled, I carry it out to the back of the truck. "I forgot *Leo the Late Bloomer*," I yell to Agatha over my shoulder. "It's her f-f-f-favorite. Can you get it?"

"You get it."

I heave the basket on the truck. "It's on the shelf in my r-r-room."

She opens the door to the truck and climbs in. "Damn, I forgot the keys."

"Get the book while you're in there," I say, taking the top layer of potatoes off the basket so I can add another book.

When Agatha gets back, she carries *The Cat in the Hat*.

I look at it, confused. "She's already read this one. I said *Leo the Late Bloomer*."

"I don't have time to fiddle around, Cornelia. I've got to get back before it gets too dark so I can get the rest of the cucumbers in from the garden. We've got to hurry."

I put *The Cat in the Hat* in the basket and cover it with potatoes.

The dogs howl as soon as we start up the driveway. The father meets us on the porch.

"What do you want?" he yells to us as soon as Agatha turns off the truck.

"You said he w-w-w-wouldn't be home."

Agatha shrugs and opens her door and climbs out. "Just had too many of these potatoes, Pete, and I was wonderin' if you could use some. We'll never use all these."

He doesn't say anything; he's looking at the back of the truck. I can tell he's trying to decide.

"Plus," Agatha hurries on, "I wanted to tell you I was sorry about your little girl. Had no business invitin' her over and all."

I can't believe she's saying that. He grumbles to himself. He finally walks off the porch and around to the back of the truck and looks at the basket of potatoes.

"All right. We'll take them." He unloads them from the truck. "Just you both stay away from my little girl, you hear?"

Everything clicks as we bounce along the road back to the house.

"You w-w-w-wouldn't have made that mistake about *Leo the Late Bloomer* if you could read."

"What you talkin' about?" Agatha looks over at me quickly. "I can read just fine." Then she laughs.

"You don't need glasses; that's not the problem," I continue, sorting out the last few loose threads. "You plant carrot seeds smaller than the head on a pin."

It all adds up. The terrible amount of work she puts into paying her bills every month, the fact that there isn't a book in the house, the way she seems more interested in Bo's reading lessons than Bo does.

"You've been on my back for w-w-w-weeks now about being scared to go back to school. Boy, you just won't give me a break. And all this time you've been hiding what a f-f-farce you are."

She doesn't say anything for a few moments as we bounce along.

"Cornelia, I don't give a rat's ass what you think. I can read just fine. I need glasses, same as I've been tellin' you since you got here."

I turn and face her. "Oh yeah? Prove it."

"The hell I will."

# 72

I know I'm a candle when I'm with Agatha now because sometimes the flame inside of me burns higher and the wax that covers me starts to melt and drip and I'm softer and lighter and I want to dance through the fields and feel the grass rub against my bare ankles.

But on other days, the days when we slam doors and scream and build fences, the flame dies out and the wax hardens, and I close up, covered by wax again, like chocolate crackle on an ice cream cone.

Another postcard arrives in early August.
This one shows a girl and her mother, arm in arm, watching
a sunrise over an early-morning ocean.

> Dear Corns,
>     Are you missing me?
>                 Love, L.

# 74

I lay the postcard on top of all the others in my dresser drawer. Six of them form a silent chain to my mother.

I rub my thumb over the newest one. I wish it had been that way: oceans and sunrises and us. Instead I am cooking by the time I turn ten. My mother has stopped working, stopped caring about anything but her newest boyfriend. I start packing my own lunches because I'm not taking free lunches from anyone. I bring egg sandwiches with ketchup, apples when we have them, and Yodels when we don't. I buy carrots and cut them into slivers and pretend they spear me like little swords, pricking at my heart as I eat them. But I am always stronger.

Agatha avoids me for the next two weeks.
I leave the phonics books I used for Bo on the table. When
the time comes for her to write her checks, she asks me to go
to the bank with her, but I say no.

When she gets back, she writes her name in the same wobbly handwriting as usual, slowly, like a child writing, and then
she angrily pushes all the bills to the floor and storms out and
I hear her start the truck and drive off.

She comes back an hour later, carrying a white paper bag.
She pulls out a large cup of coffee and hands it to me. "I
remember you used to like this."

My heart thumps.

# 76

In the end it is so simple.

"I'll go to school," I tell her as I peel a potful of turnips, "if you let me teach you to read."

We sit at Agatha's table night after night. I open *Teach Your Child to Read*.

"The letter *u* s-s-s-sounds like the *u* in *umbrella*," I say, taking another sip of sassafras. I've been drinking it for so long now that I'd almost rather have it than coffee, even though the coffee she bought me the other night was pretty good. "Now make the *u* sound. *Uh, uh, uh.*"

Agatha pushes the book on the floor. "I'm not reading this ridiculous book again." She stomps off into her room.

"B-b-b-but you have to start at the beginning," I say, picking up the book and putting it back on the table.

"I'm too old for this baby crap, Cornelia," she says, walking back into the room. "Come on, we're going to the library." She is wearing the purple hat.

Warm Milk looks at me as I walk in and smiles when she sees Agatha's hat. "Ever been in here before?" I whisper over my shoulder.

"Course not," Agatha says, stomping away from me. "Now, show me where to find a book on butterflies."

I look around for a while until I find the nature books. Agatha pulls *Butterfly Handbook* from the shelf and flips through the pages.

"Th-th-this will never work," I say.

"Why not?"

"Look at all those L-l-latin words. There's no way."

"Cornelia, if I'm going to learn to read, I'm going to do it with something I'm interested in." She grabs it back and marches over to Warm Milk's desk.

Warm Milk smiles at us. "Do you have a library card, Mrs. Thornhill?"

Agatha shakes her head.

Warm Milk pulls a couple of cards out of her drawer. "You need to sign here."

While Agatha signs her name, Warm Milk looks over at me. "If you'd like a card, I'll need your name."

I look over at the shelf where *To Kill a Mockingbird* waits for me. Agatha hands her card back to Warm Milk. But I shake my head.

Agatha looks at me and raises an eyebrow, but she doesn't say anything.

# 79

"I've been watching this tree for a long while," Agatha says on our way home. She pulls Bertha over to the side of the road and we wait until the truck sputters off. "Come on, come see." Agatha leads me to a withered tree that juts out over a stone wall. Its trunk is cracked and crossed like old veins and its bony branches reach out to half a dozen young pines that grow up around it in a dizzy circle.

Ugly tree, I think. "So?"

Agatha pokes me and laughs. "You got to look up, Cornelia. Look up!"

When I do, I see that at the very top the tree has freed itself from its bent body and burst into soft blossom. Dozens of bees buzz through its pink halo, making the slim pines crowding all around look empty-headed.

"Now there's a tree not afraid to be who it is," says Agatha.

"This isn't going to work," I say, pushing *Butterfly Handbook* toward her. Agatha takes a sip of her tea and looks at the book.

"H-h-h-how am I going to teach you the short *a* sound when all I have are w-words like *mottled dusky wing?*"

She picks up the book and flips through it for a few moments. "This, Cornelia, is a spicebush swallowtail. We'll start there."

I look down at the page. A large black butterfly with orange and yellow spots at the edge of its wings sits above the words *spicebush swallowtail*.

"How did you read that?" I ask, unbelieving.

"I know what they *look* like, Cornelia. I've seen them since I was a little girl on this farm. Now if I know what they look like, with your help, I should be able to figure out the word. I've just been needin' someone to help me put all the sounds together, that's all.

"Now, let's get started," she says, popping a sugar cube into her mouth. "I don't have all day."

# 81

Several weeks later, we bake blueberry pies and Agatha slowly reads the ingredients while I measure. "When are you goin' to keep up your end of the bargain?" she asks me between the words *sugar* and *cinnamon*.

She doesn't know that I can't. Since the last postcard, I'm sure my mother will come for me.

On Saturday, I wake to the clanging of pots and pans. Agatha ignores me when I walk into the kitchen. Dirty dishes and mixing spoons and a pile of cake pans cover my clean counter.

"What are you doing?"

"Making lemon cake."

She never cooks. "What for?" I wonder how long it will take to scrape the hardening flour paste that clumps along the edge of the kitchen sink.

"To celebrate."

"Celebrate what?"

"The woods."

"The woods?" She is nuts. "N-n-no thanks."

I leave the mess and walk outside to wait for my mother.

# 83

As the moon rises, Agatha approaches the front step. I knot myself deeper inside myself. She walks up to me with a blanket under her arm, a cake in her hands, and a jug of something to drink over her shoulder. She wears her hat.

"Are you coming?"

"No. I don't want to celebrate the woods. That's ridiculous."

"I'm celebratin' what smart women have always known. A night in the woods is medicine for the heart."

She's been eating too many turnips, I'm sure. "I'm not coming."

"Your choice." She turns away and walks toward the fields behind the house. I watch her disappear into the darkness.

When I find her half an hour later, she's eaten half the cake.

"Come closer," she whispers. "I want to show you something over this slope."

Immediately, I see why she has come. Hundreds of tiny

lights zip and blink through the night. Fireflies by the hundreds soar and flit and light up the sky on this starless night.

"Lightning bugs," she says. "City folks call them fireflies, but up here we call them lightning bugs."

"They're amazing!" I say, sitting on the blanket beside her.

"They're the perfect insect, you know." She cuts a slice of lemon cake and hands it to me.

"How so?"

"Well, they don't bite, they don't attack, they don't carry disease, and they're not poisonous. All they do is fly around and put on a show. They're looking for mates."

"How do you kn-kn-know all that?"

"I've been reading about them." I think she might be grinning in the darkness.

I smile. "Wh-what else do you know about them?"

"It's not electricity that lights them up. It's a chemical inside them. It helps them find each other."

We watch them for a while. I wonder when my mother will find me.

I take a sip of the drink. It tastes sweet and thick. "She's coming back."

Agatha sighs. "Maybe she knows something you don't— that she can't take care of you right now."

The air feels thin and flat. "She's coming back," I whisper again.

"Maybe she's not ready." She pours something from the jug into my cup. "Here, have some."

"What is it, anyway?"

"It's cider, lemon, strawberries, and whipped cream. We

143

always called it syllabub. It'll sweeten you up, Cornelia." She laughs a low, sweet melody.

I give her my most sour look, but I don't think she can see it in the darkness.

"Maybe she's not ready," she says again. "Your ma's like a butterfly that comes out of its chrysalis too soon. Know what happens then?"

I shake my head, certain I don't want to hear.

"Butterflies get strong in the struggle. If you help it out of its chrysalis, it doesn't get to struggle and it's too weak to fly on its own. Your ma, she keeps looking for the easy way out."

## 84

Bo walks into the kitchen one day while I am sautéing tofu and garlic. "Are you supposed to be here?"

"He's back at work."

"Well, you still shouldn't come. Did your m-m-m-mother have the baby?"

Bo smiles. "A girl. I've been reading to her." She reaches down beside her. "Here, I brought these back. Do you have any more?"

I look at *The Cat in the Hat.* "You could just go to the library. You have your own card now."

"Yes, but you know which ones to pick, Corney."

I turn off the heat under the frying pan. "You're going to n-n-n-need harder ones now." I walk into my room and pull *Harriet the Spy* out of my top drawer. "It's hard, but you'll really love it, Bo."

She puts it into her backpack.

"Where's Agatha?"

"Out in the woods. Doing whatever it is she does with those trees."

"Haven't you asked her yet?"

Frankly, I didn't give it much thought anymore. I've been too busy counting the days to my birthday.

"You should go see, Corney, you really should."

## 85

When Bo leaves, I follow the path that Agatha's moccasins have worn into the grass this summer. The path begins at old Esther, who has lost a window again. From there, the trail passes the barn and winds into the woods and stops at a tepee.

The saplings that she has stripped of branches and bark through the summer now stand in the shade of a towering oak. The tepee is twice my height; pine boughs cover and blanket the outside in deep mossy green.

"It's beautiful," I say as Agatha walks out of the woods with her arms filled with pine needles. She stops when she sees me, smiles, and then walks up and pours her armload of needles inside. When she crawls back out, she grins.

"It's for you," she says. "Sometimes a person needs a cocoon for a while."

I bend down and peek in through the opening: pine needles mound into a thick mattress. My eyes fill with tears as I crawl inside.

# 86

I spend so much time in my tepee, the month of October passes with me inside. I cover the pine needles with blankets and lie down and look up at the long thin poles and the way Agatha has stripped them of their bark. That gets me to thinking about stripping my own bark.

One morning after I wash the breakfast dishes, I take one of the notebooks I bought for Bo. I lie back and look up at the way Agatha has interlocked the poles at the top of the tepee, and I think about my life. Then I write *My Life, Chapter One* on the cover.

I open to the first page and my words fly. I forget everything I know about poetic meter and active voice and the right word and the not-so-right word because my words come too fast and too furious to slow down.

I write the story of my mother's leaving. It wasn't like one day she was here and the next day she left. It's like one day she left a little. And then the next day she left a little more. And then she started falling asleep on the couch instead of hugging me. I would crawl up with her and put her arms around me and snuggle against her. But that's when I was little. Later, her arms got thin and then it didn't feel so safe anymore.

I prayed a lot then. *Please make my mother not leave me.* But God didn't listen. Why?

And then I write the story of me leaving myself. I remember when I started stuttering. It wasn't like one day I didn't stutter and then one day I did. It was one day I stuttered just a little. And then I got scared and the next day I stuttered a little more. Before I knew it I was stuttering all the time. I started noticing that when I stuttered, people looked away. That hurt worse than the stuttering, so I started looking away from myself. I'd look at my feet, the ground, the floor because I was too scared to look them in the eyes. I stopped talking. I got too scared to try.

When I was eight, I began to pray, *Please, God, help me not stutter.* But God didn't listen. Why?

Now I live with Agatha. She's built me this tepee that I spend hours inside each day. I pray my mother will come, but my birthday comes and goes with no sign of her. God still isn't listening. Why?

And then I cry. The wound in my throat finally lets go.

A pile of rubble sits outside my tepee door. The branches Agatha cut off the poles, the bark, the leaves she raked before she began construction, the dirt she cleared to level the ground, all this she left in a wide pile about six feet from the door.

Usually I march right past, ignoring another of her messes, but today as I climb out into the light, my face still wet, I notice something new.

A tiny woodland flower grows up out of the ruins, so delicate and wispy it could be a white fairy reaching for the sun. The stem is slim as a strand of spaghetti, and it wobbles a bit, but it dances a rhythm all its own as the pines sway above.

It waves to me as I kneel down and touch its little face.

Warm Milk looks up at me as I put *To Kill a Mockingbird* on the counter.

"Do you have a library card?"

I shake my head.

"You've been in here before, haven't you?" She smiles at me and I nod.

"Well, then. It will only take a minute." She turns to her computer. "Your name, please?"

Think about anything, *anything* else, I tell myself. They used to kill saints in all sorts of horrible ways; think about that. My mother told me this during one of her "why are you wasting a perfectly good afternoon sitting in an empty church" speeches. They stoned them and burned them and dunked them in hot oil and pressed them. Pressing is when they made someone lie on the ground and they put a board on top of them and then they put stones on, one at a time, until the person died.

Tell my heart it is not being pressed right now, I think.

Warm Milk looks up at me again. "I need your name."

"Ah-ah-ah-ah." I press my foot into the floor. "C-c-c . . ." I stop, start over. "C-c-cornelia Th-th-th-thornhill." I look down, then force my eyes up. Warm Milk is not looking away.

## 89

I walk up the church steps, open the door, and step into a quiet that covers and draws me to a middle pew. A candle burns inside a glass globe. We are alone, the candle and I. Sun pours through the windows and sends shards of greens and blues and yellows across my skin. The windows each depict a scene from the Bible. I don't really know what they mean. It doesn't matter. I come for the quiet. A snowflake striking pavement would make more noise than I hear in this church.

I do this a lot now, stop in on my way home from the library, now that I have a library card. I think it's awfully nice that they leave the door unlocked. One of these days, if someone asks what I'm doing, I could say I'm trying to figure out if my mother was right when she said only fools and hypocrites come to church. Maybe people who go to a place like this are just trying to make sense of things. Maybe they come here because when they do, they start to feel better.

I feel kind of soft in the center, kind of peaceful, kind of free. Who knows, maybe my head's all foggy from the incense that hangs over everything. That's what my mother would say. But I get the feeling she'd be wrong.

Most of my life I have been a bird tethered to the ground, my speech the leather strap that binds me to earth. But as I sit here in the silence, I feel the tethers loosen, and I can almost fly.

We sit in the truck across the street from the high school as a bus pulls up and the door squeaks open.

"I'll go with you." Agatha buttons her coat and straightens her hat. The hat seems bigger, more purple this morning.

"No," I say quickly. "I'll be all right." But I don't move. Students begin walking up the steps to the school, past a man wearing a blue suit and tie, probably the principal, and through a set of glass doors and into the school.

Everyone carries a backpack. I look down at Agatha's canvas sack that sits on my lap and I sigh.

"I put a sandwich in there," Agatha says, turning to me.

I have forgotten lunch. I pull out a sandwich wrapped in a blue bandanna. I unwrap it and lift a corner of the whole wheat bread, sniffing for mushrooms or fiddleheads.

"Don't worry." She laughs. "It's just cheese."

"Can I help you?" says a woman in the office who finally puts down her telephone and walks up to me.

"I w-w-w-want to come to s-s-school here." It takes all my courage to look at her as I try to explain why I have no transcript. I don't tell her that my mother pulled me out of ninth grade when the school year was nearly over. "I'm a sophomore."

"Well," she says, "I just don't know."

As I'm finishing, the man who stood at the steps walks into the office. Hearing what I'm trying to say, he asks, "Where are you from?"

"N-n-n-n-new York." I'm still looking up, even when he looks away.

"You better put her in Mrs. Paul's room."

"In this school we reach for the stars," he says as I pick my sack up off the floor. "Are you ready to do that?"

I feel myself begin to bloom from deep inside as I walk down the hall.

"Th-th-these are the books I've r-r-r-read," I say a week later, slapping a paper on my English teacher's desk. I've written down the titles of all the books I've read over the last few years that already meet the sophomore honors English requirements. *To Kill a Mockingbird, A Separate Peace, Jane Eyre, Wuthering Heights.* She scans it for a moment, then looks up.

"Very nice, dear," she says, stuffing a wad of Kleenex into the cuff of her sleeve. "Now go have a seat."

I don't move. I've sat through this class day after day and each day grows worse. "I've read all of these b-b-b-books already. I should not be r-r-reading this." I dump her watered-down *Tom Sawyer* on her desk. "Besides, I've already r-r-r-read this one."

She looks up at the class and skims the paper again quickly, then hands the paper back to me. "Have a seat, Cornelia. We're going to read aloud today."

I grab the paper. I leave the book on her desk and walk back to my seat.

The first boy begins. " 'The adventure of the day tormented Tom's dreams that night.' " No one listens. A boy with his sneakers untied flicks a paper clip at a girl in the back of the room. Mrs. Paul doesn't notice. I wonder how the boy reading feels about being in this class. He reads straight and even, a pressed shirt. Maybe if they gave the kids in this class *real* literature, they'd want to read when they got home and we wouldn't have to read out loud like babies.

A girl begins to read. " 'The next afternoon Tom and Huck met down by the river to plan their strategy.' "

I'm so furious and so hopeless as the next boy begins. I'm next. It's always the same. There's the buildup. I know what's coming. The faces will look at me when the words get caught in my throat, wondering what's taking so long. And then they will turn away.

When my turn comes, I look out the window.

## 93

I get called to the principal's office halfway through lunch. The principal and my English teacher wait for me at a table in the office.

"Mrs. Paul says you refuse to read in her class."

I nod.

"Why would that be?" The principal wears the blue suit. I wonder if he has any others. I shrug.

"Is it because of your stuttering?"

I shrug again. It's pointless. Already they think they know everything about me.

"We have a speech therapist who comes once a week from Dover. We would like her to evaluate you."

I nod.

"Very well. Any questions?" He's looking at me, waiting.

I shake my head.

He stands and waits for me to go. When I look up at him, his eyes tell me, *Problem solved*. But the problem isn't solved. I'm angry enough to spit nails into his teeth, but I'm afraid to open my mouth.

What about the honors class? I want him to talk about *that*. But I'm caught in the space between what I want to say and knowing I can't. *Or what I think I can't.*

I stand, too. And then I pull the reading list from my pocket and throw it in front of him. "I have read *W-w-wuthering H-h-h-heights* and you have me reading *Tom Sawyer* for b-b-b-babies. I should be in the honors cl-cl-class."

He looks away. "Well, lots of kids think they should be in the honors class." He looks from the clock on the wall to the class ring on his finger and he twists it back and forth. "Let's see how you do in Mrs. Paul's room for a while and then we'll move you up if you can do the work."

I know how this plays out. You never move. *Nevermore. Quoth the Raven, "Nevermore."*

"N-n-n-no."

He raises an eyebrow.

"Hush now," says Mrs. Paul.

I push her words aside. "I have r-r-r-read these b-b-b-b-books." I push the paper closer to him.

He sits back down and reads them all.

"But you have no transcript. Has it arrived?" He looks up at the secretary, who walked into his office when she heard the fuss. She shakes her head.

"This is quite a list." He looks at me. "How do I know you've really read them?"

"Q-q-quiz me."

"Okay," he says, "*Wuthering Heights*. Main character?"

"H-h-h-heathcliff and Catherine."

"Conflict?"

160

"Heathcliff l-l-l-loves Catherine, but she m-m-m-marries someone else."

"Time period?"

"Early eighteen hundreds."

He turns to Mrs. Paul. "Is this right?"

She shrugs. "I think so. It's been a long time."

He turns to the secretary. "Call Mr. Browne down here." He taps his pencil while we wait. Mr. Browne doesn't hurry. We sit for ten minutes and wait. *Tap. Tap. Tap.*

When Mr. Browne finally walks into the room, he is licking an ice cream sandwich and two drops of vanilla run down his tie and he doesn't notice.

The principal tells him my answers. Mr. Browne nods and smiles over at me. "Yes, it is quite challenging, wouldn't you say?" I grin. There are little snowmen rolling all over his tie. When he sits down, I see he's wearing Christmas socks.

The principal looks down the list. *"To Kill a Mockingbird?"*

"Scout and her brother, J-j-jem, are the m-m-m-main characters, and their father, Atticus Finch, is important, too."

"Conflict?"

"Whether p-p-people are good or evil underneath it all." I glare at Mrs. Paul. "Also, it's about what happens when pr-pr-prejudice goes wild."

The honors teacher looks over at me. "She's right." He reaches for the list. "Have you read all these books?"

His voice reminds me of Warm Milk's at the library, only it's heavier, lumpier, but comforting, like mashed potatoes. I want to tell him my story. I look up at him. "Yes," I say.

"Very well and good," says the principal. "But we don't have any transcript." He yells to the secretary. "Have you called down there yet?"

She begins dialing the phone.

I press my foot into the floor so hard that it cramps. But I don't look down. I look at the principal. "No. I'm n-not going back to that class."

A few seconds of empty space hang awkwardly before Mr. Browne leans forward. "Why don't we try her in my class and see how she does?"

I bloom a little more from the spot deep inside myself. I am a chrysanthemum, a late bloomer, a fall bloomer, a bloomer nonetheless.

# 94

A pot of cinnamon and cloves and apples steams on the woodstove one Saturday morning when I walk into the kitchen wearing my warmest socks. Agatha sits at the table, a cup of sassafras in front of her. I take a cup from the cupboard and fill it with sassafras and sit on the wooden chair beside her.

The tiny sweater that I found under the bed all those months ago sits on her lap. She runs her fingers over the buttons and along the lace that edges the neck.

"I've stayed away from the mountain for too long," she says, running her fingers along the delicate stitches without looking up. "It's been years. Want to go with me?"

I sip my tea. I haven't thought about the mountain in a long time. I don't want to escape so badly now that I have a tepee.

"It's pretty cold out there," I say, grateful for my socks. "When are you going?" I take a large slurp of the sassafras. It warms me deeper now than coffee.

"I was waiting for you to get up." She rubs the sweater against her cheek. "No snow in the air, not today. We can make it to the top and back if we get going."

## 95

"Look down there, Cornelia." I follow Agatha's finger back along the fields we have just climbed behind her house. I cinch my coat tighter.

"It's Thornhill land. All of it. And up there, too. Several hundred acres."

"The mountain's yours, too?" It stretches high in the distance.

Agatha laughs. "You been callin' it a mountain since you got here. It's not much more than a hill. But yes, it's ours."

Agatha's breath wisps out of her mouth in cloudy puffs. "They been wantin' our land for years, but I hold on and on. Some years I have a phone, some I don't."

She walks up to a stone wall and sits down and I open the canvas sack and reach in for the cheese, muffins, and apples I've packed for us.

"Is it wo-wo-worth it if you can't have a phone?" I pour two cups of sassafras tea from the thermos. Agatha pulls a couple of sugar lumps from her overalls and pops them into her cup.

"You tell me. Look around you."

White feathery ice glistens in the oaks now that the leaves have fallen. Thigh-high grass tilts in the cold wind. White pine and spruce, oaks and maples march up the sides of the hill into the distance. The sky is the thin blue color of the water in the brook.

"I could sell some of it off, like some of our neighbors want. Moss wants the wood. Others wanted to put a golf course here once, but we Thornhills have always known that land is the one thing you never sell. Because with land you got a place for your roots to go down deep."

I think about my mother. She never got her roots down deep. Is that it? I wonder why having me wasn't enough to make her want to get root-bound. I wonder if the boyfriend is enough.

"There's one thing that would get me to sell some of it off," she says after taking a loud finishing slurp of her tea, putting the cup back into the pack, and standing up. "Sendin' you to college. Bo's right. You read better than anyone, Cornelia. There's a big enough piece across the street to get you started, anyway."

I am speechless and it's not because I'm afraid to talk. I reach over and hug her for the first time ever and when I do, she hugs me back.

We climb again and leave the fields and walk into a beech forest. I follow Agatha and listen to her moccasins pad quietly up the hill, past the tall straight trunks of the trees covered with bark as smooth and tight as young elephant skin. We pass

166

another brook and I stop for a drink, feel the water alive on my tongue.

Agatha's steps slow as we get closer to the top and I wonder if her feet are getting cold. She wears the moccasins summer and winter; she just adjusts the number and thickness of socks to the weather. I slow down, too, matching my pace to hers so that we walk side by side. Then she slows even more and I start wondering about her age. Just how old is she? I've never asked; she's never told me. I've seen her carry bushels of turnips and potatoes, one after the other without stopping. She's the first one up in the morning, the last one to bed at night. I know she's solid as her own land, but she is definitely slowing down. The skin on her face looks tight, drawn.

"Are you all right?"

"Fine, I'm fine. I just need to sit down for a bit."

"You don't l-l-l-look too well." I pour another cup of tea.

She drinks quickly, hands the mug back to me, and I refill it.

"I haven't been here in a long time. You make me remember things. Come on, let's get going."

Agatha's steps slow and then she stops. Tears puddle in her eyes. "What's the matter?" I say, alarmed. This isn't like Agatha, oak that she is.

"I stayed away from here for a long time, Cornelia. That's all."

As we walk on, I see that the crest of the hill is surrounded by a grove of pines. There's an opening, a doorway, and sun pours into the space in heavy drapes. Agatha quickens her step

and walks into the space, a sanctuary in the woods, and I follow.

A wooden cross stands in the center.

## GRACE THORNHILL
## 1960–1961

Agatha kneels beside the cross and pulls the tiny sweater
from the pocket of her coat and lays it on her lap, along with
the mittens, hat, and booties. She rubs them and closes her
eyes. Tears stream down her face.

"Some things always hurt," she says after a while.

"You bu-bu-buried her up here?" I whisper. "It's b-b-b-
beautiful."

"No. They buried her near the hospital. Her spirit's here,
though. I made sure of that."

"I'm sorry."

Agatha looks over at me. "I didn't dump her off, as you
said that day."

I wish she wouldn't get into that fight we had all those
months ago. Everything just hurt so much then.

"The doctor told me that no woman by herself could take
care of a child that sick, that Grace would be better off in a
hospital. I didn't argue, I didn't know any better. I was young
and foolish and didn't speak up. I have been sorry about that
every day of my life."

"It's so t-tiny," I say, looking down at the sweater.

"Took me half a year. I kept ripping it apart and starting

over. But she wore it. It was winter when she was born." She rubs the sweater on her cheek.

"I'm sorry," I say again.

"Me too. Lots of pain in life. Lots more joy. You got to find a way to stand through both."

## 96

One day in early December, Agatha and I drive back from the library with a pile of books between us. Agatha's *Bird Behavior* rests on top.

Snowflakes flit through the yard as I look across at my mother, huddled under her coat, on the front step. Half a year—it sure took you long enough is all I can think.

"Hi, Corns." My mother stands up when I walk over. Her arms hang skinnier, if that's possible.

"What are you d–d–d–doing here?" I step forward, unsure, but my heart is leaping.

"Seeing you, you goose." She laughs in that nervous way that scrapes at bone. She nods as Agatha walks up behind me. I am getting used to the quiet scuff of my aunt's moccasins. I had forgotten how she towers over my mother. Same thin wrists, but an oak and a sapling.

"Where's the ride?" my aunt says finally.

"At the store to get some things."

"I knew you'd come back," I whisper, stepping closer.

My mother looks at her feet, then steps forward and hugs

me the way a little boy hugs his mother when his friends are watching. Her dress floats loose under her coat as she steps back. Her cowboy boots barely leave a print in the snow.

I want to give her a fat slice of whole wheat bread with a thick spread of molasses, some cheese, and a chunk of apple pie to keep her from fading away.

"I missed you real bad, Corns." She looks up at me quickly and I see the hesitancy in her eyes in the instant before she blinks it away. "We're going to Atlantic City, Corns. I'll come get you soon as I can."

My spine straightens and hardens as anger rises from deep inside. I clamp my teeth down over my climbing fury, imagining myself getting real heavy, folding over onto myself, getting thick so her words can't reach the spot deep inside that hasn't turned hard yet. And I'm trying harder than I've ever tried before as my mother keeps glancing out at the road for the boyfriend's car.

But it's not working. My mother lights a cigarette and I notice the Yodels package sticking out of her pocket. I unclamp my teeth. I've spent so much time in the tepee, so much time with Agatha, that when I push the anger down now, all I want is a voice.

"We won't be there long before we come get you. Just long enough to get settled and get jobs and stuff."

My aunt touches my shoulder. My mother looks off to the road. She smokes her cigarette in short quick drags, and I watch her shoulders slump and I see her pain and then, like a gush from a vein, I feel mine.

"Maybe things will finally start working out for us," she

says while looking out at the road. "You can go to school down there, Corns."

She keeps on talking, stumbling along about the way it will be for us someday, but this time, as the tears fall down my face, I look away from her.

I think about that day I began writing about my life in the tepee and how I promised myself I would never hide again. I watch my mother explain how she'll come back for me, how I can practically count the days on my fingers, she'll come back so soon. Never hide my face, I told myself that day, never again. Never look at my feet, never again.

I look up at Agatha, then back to my mother. "I'll b–b–b– be okay here."

My mother looks away. But I walk across the miles and miles that stretch between us and hug her anyway.

"I bet I owe a huge fine," I say as I wrap a brown paper bag around the library's copy of *Oliver Twist* that I tucked in my drawer all those months ago. "Here, hold this string."

Agatha puts her book, *Foraging for Wild Foods,* on the counter. Just the title makes me shudder. She pushes her finger on the string and I tie a tight bow.

"Send 'em a jar of fiddleheads. Bet they'd appreciate that in the city."

"That's the l-l-looniest thing I've ever heard," I say, picking up a pen and writing our return address in bold black letters.

We climb the mountain a lot come spring.
We bring our books and cheese sandwiches and a thermos of
sassafras. We give Grace lots of attention because it makes us
both feel better. We call it tending to Grace.

Agatha opens a jar of fiddleheads one warm day in May
and sticks her fork into the jar. Watching her, I think about
how there was a time when I wanted an aunt in an apron
with flour on her cheek. Instead I got an old woman who eats
fiddleheads and rarely cleans her house. I didn't get what I was
looking for, not at all. But I did get an old woman who knows
the best fireworks hide in the tails of hundreds of lightning
bugs.

She chomps away on the fiddleheads and makes them
look almost edible, then licks her fork clean.

"Did you know," she says, "there are twelve thousand
kinds of ferns? They're still finding new ones."

"How m-m-many are edible?" I ask, digging a hole and
planting a ring of daisies.

"These sure are." She pokes her fork into the jar again and laughs until she hiccups.

"Are you sure?" I ask, leaning closer. "They don't look it to me."

"I'm sure." She licks her fork again. "I haven't fallen down dead yet."

She takes another forkful and munches it peacefully, then takes another, and another after that. I wonder what she thinks about. Maybe Grace. Maybe my mother. Maybe me.

"Can I try some of those?" I say after watching her awhile.

She gives me an odd look, but she hands me the jar. I stick my fork in and catch a clump and put it on my tongue—and spit it out immediately.

"They're awful!" I roll over, gagging. Fiddleheads taste cold and bitter, like wet nails.

Agatha laughs so hard she falls back in the grass. "Fiddleheads ain't for everybody," she says, her sides heaving.

"N-n-n-neither are you," I say while trying to wipe the fiddleheads from my tongue with the back of my hand.

She laughs even harder then, and I start laughing, too. I laugh harder and harder until I flop over on my back and hold my stomach and the tears roll down my face and nearly choke me.

"Neither are you," I say after I can breathe again, and my voice grows strong and deep and I don't look away.

## ACKNOWLEDGMENTS

With grateful appreciation to: my mother and father, for encouraging my writing from the very beginning; my editor, Michelle Frey, who believed Cornelia had a voice to share; my husband, Steven, who rooted for Cornelia from the first day he met her; and my children, Daniel, Matthew, Kate, and Laura, the brightest stars ever to shine on my life. Thank you.